T0147676

PEMBROKE

The Adventures of
Arthur Bacterium and Patty Virus

PEMBROKE

The Adventures of
Arthur Bacterium and Patty Virus

Taylor Samuel Lyen

iUniverse, Inc.
Bloomington

Pembroke
The Adventures of Arthur Bacterium and Patty Virus

Copyright © 2012 by Taylor Samuel Lyen

All rights reserved. No part of this book may be used or reproduced by
any means, graphic, electronic, or mechanical, including photocopying,
recording, taping or by any information storage retrieval system
without the written permission of the publisher except in the case
of brief quotations embodied in critical articles and reviews.

iUniverse books may be ordered through booksellers or by contacting:

iUniverse
1663 Liberty Drive
Bloomington, IN 47403
www.iuniverse.com
1-800-Authors (1-800-288-4677)

Because of the dynamic nature of the Internet, any web addresses or links
contained in this book may have changed since publication and may no longer be
valid. The views expressed in this work are solely those of the author and do not
necessarily reflect the views of the publisher, and the publisher hereby disclaims
any responsibility for them.

Any people depicted in stock imagery provided by Thinkstock are
models, and such images are being used for illustrative purposes only.
Certain stock imagery © Thinkstock.

ISBN: 978-1-4759-5855-3 (sc)

ISBN: 978-1-4759-5856-0 (e)

Printed in the United States of America

iUniverse rev. date: 11/13/2012

Dedicated to the wondrously curious and
ever-questioning natures of
Austin and Megan, my grandchildren. Your lives are
so precious to me. You have shown me the way to love
and appreciate everything at a much deeper level.

Crapa

CONTENTS

ACKNOWLEDGMENTS

MY THANKS to Ben Sugman, Connie Deitrick, Effie Kontonicas, Gina West, Isabel Sanchez, Jack McKay, Kimberly Adams, Larry Crans, Nancy Ustaszewski, and Robin Olivier for reading the rough draft of *Pembroke* and providing me with valuable feedback.

My appreciation and thanks go to Edith Gutterres, executive director of Raskob Learning Institute and Day School, Holy Names University, Oakland; Stefani Wulkan, lead teacher and assistant director; and Polly Mayer, clinical director, for their assessment of *Pembroke*'s readability and comprehension levels and their review of the book and suggestions for improvement.

Commenting on the manuscript from the perspective of an artist and educator, Dr. Adeyinka Fashokun of Graphsedifix: Enlightenment through Visual Arts and administrator, Mount Diablo Unified School District, generously gave of his time and talent to review the manuscript, for which I am thankful.

Christopher Livanos, associate professor of University of Wisconsin Department of Comparative

Literature, was kind enough to read the book and give it a thumbs-up, although, he commented, "One suggestion is that a little scatological humor goes a long way. I think it could be pared back just a little more. One reference to the green goo at the Sphincter of Oddi gets the point across."

Dr. Richard Barrett, DVM, Canyon Veterinary Hospital, Castro Valley California, assured me that my science is plausible and accurate as far as the anatomy and physiology of small dogs are concerned. His insights, humorous comments, and contributions are always welcome.

Last, but certainly not least, I'd like to thank Pat Parker, science teacher, and Lynn Tierney, chemistry teacher, at Castro Valley High School, who know the value of an adventuresome summer vacation. They read the book from secondary science teachers' perspectives and provided excellent suggestions.

CREDITS

Front page photo from Shutterstock Images. (Pembroke, a Welsh corgi, sitting on South Port with a smile on his face.)

Back cover author photo by Effie Enterprises Photography.

Dedication page photo of grandchildren by Kimberly Adams, Austin and Megan's mother.

Diagram of Dog drawn by Professor Bacterium, showing the points traveled in the Adventures of Arthur Bacterium and Patty Virus.

Inside author photo by Marie Helen Castellanos. (Author, a sixth-grade teacher at Sydney Elementary School in the Castro Valley Unifi ed School District.)

Note: A glossary and pronunciation guide follows the story. Definitions and pronunciation of words are based on the Microsoft Word for Mac version 11.6.0 dictionary and thesaurus; Wikipedia, the free online encyclopedia; and on Webster's New World Dictionary, Third College Edition, n, Prentice Hall (1994).

Prologue

PEMBROKE

It's a beautiful, dreamy summer's day as Pembroke romps out of the backdoor of his home into the large backyard to play fetch with Jimmy Monroe. Jimmy picks up Pembroke's favorite stick and hurls it over the apricot tree. Pembroke scuttles as fast as his short legs can carry him to the spot where the stick lands. He snaps it up in his mouth and scurries back to Jimmy. Within seconds, the stick sails in the air again, striking the top of the garbage can, and bouncing into the vegetable patch. Pembroke motors through the vegetables, fetches the stick, and dutifully returns it to Jimmy. Every morning Pembroke plays fetch with his young master until his short, furry body lies exhausted in the cool green grass. His water and food bowls are filled before Jimmy leaves for school. Jimmy lovingly pets Pembroke and tells him to be a good dog until he gets back.

Jimmy leaves and Pembroke naps, as is his usually habit. Hearing something move near the swimming pool, he squirms over, rolls to his feet, and shuttles to the pool. A blue belly lizard darts into a leaf pile; Pembroke gives full pursuit. After unsuccessfully nosing through the dead foliage, he loses interest. Standing up, Pembroke surveys his domain. He is left to play all day in the Monroe backyard, happily exploring his world until Jimmy's return.

Pembroke is the center of his own universe. He sleeps in the Monroe's house on Jimmy's bed. He goes on every family vacation. He is fed the best foods. His fur is healthy and brushed often. In his entire life, Pembroke has never felt the bite of even one flea. In return, Pembroke faithfully obeys his masters' commands. He curls up by each family member every chance he gets. He places his head in their laps and lovingly looks at them with his brown languid eyes. He is petted and fussed over and talked to constantly. On occasion he joins in the conversations, but usually, he is content to sit tall and listen attentively. Pembroke is the most loving and loyal and protective dog any family could hope for.

Now seven years old, nothing escapes Pembroke's keen eyesight or his senses of smell and taste and sound—nothing, that is, except for the small universe constantly abuzz within him. Yes, from time to time Pembroke's stomach may rumble and some days he may feel out of sorts, but he has no idea of what's really going on inside of him. He has no idea of the countless lives that depend on him: the trillions and trillions of microorganisms living in his fur, on his skin, or enclosed within his body.

Chapter 1

DAYDREAM

ARTHUR BACTERIUM is almost nine hours old and goes to the best school in Pembroke: Pepsin Academy. He is a bright, good-looking lavender rod-shaped bacterium, who will soon attend Der Kot University, where his father and mother teach. Today he sits at his desk in his fourth grade class and looks through the window at the playground where millions and millions of kindergarten bacteria play on the jungle gym equipment and the big slide. Arthur watches his colorful rod-shaped and spherical-shaped bacteria brothers and sisters and cousins climb to the top of the ladder and tumble over each other as they stream down the long, curvy slide. Bacteria of all colors slide down and bounce off the inside of Pembroke's colon wall. Pembroke, however, does not feel the kindergarteners sliding and playing

1

and bouncing because bacteria are very small and weigh less than a dust particle.

Arthur's large brown eyes wander toward the river that passes by Pepsin Academy. He wonders what it would be like to travel upstream to the source of the river. His father has told him that the source of the Great Brown River begins where Pembroke's stomach dumps digested food into the small intestine. He stares at a map of Pembroke's digestive system that is on the wall of his classroom and plans a make-believe journey to the river's source. As one thought wanders to another, Arthur's daydream shifts to his birthday party. He knows his mother and father, grandparents and great-grandparents, aunts and uncles, and cousins will be there. He can always count on his family. He knows Ace, his best friend, will be there. He can count on his good friends—Polly, Casey, Al, Amy, Sal, and Biff. But who else will be there from school? Who will surprise him from the neighborhood? Arthur is so engrossed in his birthday party daydream, he's clueless that his teacher has started the class.

"Good morning, boys and girls. We have a new student joining us today. Let me introduce Patty—Patty Virus," announces Mrs. Lactose, Arthur's classroom teacher.

Arthur's classmates look at Patty and gasp in horror. How did a virus ever move to Southern Pembroke? How did she ever get into Pepsin Academy? Patty does not look anything like the millions of beautiful geometric rod-shaped and spherical-shaped blue, green, lavender, or red colored bacteria in their class. She looks like a bugged-eyed blob with orange spikes sticking out. But all the whoop-de-do and horror about the new girl in class doesn't draw Arthur away from his thoughts.

"Patty, you can use the desk by the window for now. Arthur, would you like to help Patty with her books and help her set up for class?"

Hearing his name called through the dreamy fog, Arthur smartly snaps out of his trance and stands to attention by his desk, answering, "Yes, Mrs. Lactose."

As might be expected, Arthur doesn't have the slightest idea about what his teacher said or what she wants from him. So he simply stands there, waiting for the teacher to repeat herself.

"Well, Arthur, go ahead and help Patty."

Arthur looks at the orange feathery sphere—who is only about the size of a bacterium's volleyball—standing beside the teacher. Patty smiles. Suddenly Arthur feels emotions tingling through his lavender rod-shaped body like he's never felt before. He's warm all over, almost like he's coming down with the flu. In his eyes, Patty is as cute as Tinker Bell—without the wings, of course. Her pixie face and large almond-shaped brown eyes wondrously peer out from under her long eyelashes, spellbinding him. She is small enough for him to hold in his hands.

"Yes, Mrs. Lactose," Arthur answers.

Millions of his classmates' disbelieving stares follow Arthur as he walks across the room. They watch him collect schoolbooks and give Patty pencils, paper, a ruler, and a brand new compass. His classmates see Arthur give her one of his favorite blue pencils and a brand new eraser from his own pencil box. Then, to his classmates' amazement, Arthur gives Patty a Sassy McFrassy Sparkle Folder! Arthur's classmates are envious as they watch Patty place her belongings in her new Sassy McFrassy Folder.

"So far, class," the teacher opens the morning lesson, "we have reviewed our year's work in history, literature, and science," Mrs. Lactose proudly says, reminding her students of their accomplishments.

The children have a difficult time splitting their attention between hearing their teacher's instructions and trying to hear what orange Patty and lavender Arthur are whispering to each other. Arthur is one of the most handsome and popular boys at school; why would he have any interest in a virus? Unaware that she has lost the attention of her class, Mrs. Lactose drones on with her lesson.

"With only four days of school left before summer vacation, we need to finish reviewing what we have learned in mathematics this year. Let's start with the *probability* and *statistics* questions on page two hundred ten."

"Oh! Oh!" Millions of hands go up as the bacteria strain to get the teacher's attention.

"Colin," the teacher says, picking on the only student in the class not raising a hand, "give me an example of what the terms *probable* and *improbable* mean."

"Until now," Colin replies, "I would have said the chance of Arthur falling in love with an ugly virus is *improbable*, but now it seems to be certain."

The classes' booming laughter draws a stern look from Mrs. Lactose, who thinks the class laughed because Colin wrongly answered her question, not using the word *probable* in his response.

"Now, class!" Mrs. Lactose waits until the class quiets and refocuses their full attention on her before continuing, "Colin's answer is a good try. I don't want anyone to not answer my questions because he or she is afraid of making a mistake."

Standing stiff as a board and wide-eyed, Colin doesn't know what to make of the teacher's comment.

"Colin," Mrs. Lactose says gently, "if someone *seems to be certain*, then he or she is said to be *probably certain*. Please use the word *probable* in your answer, dear."

The class laughs again, this time more quietly. When the teacher looks at her students, the laughter stops.

As Colin's mind works as fast as it can, time seems to stand still. Finally he says, "Yes, Mrs. Lactose. It is *probable* that Arthur is head over heels in love with an ugly virus."

"Very good, Colin, you may be seated," Mrs. Lactose replies.

An embarrassed Arthur whispers, "I'm sorry for Colin's rudeness, Patty. His grandfather started this school, so Colin thinks he's a big shot."

"That's okay. I'm used to being made fun of by others. They think I am a bad virus. They don't understand that I am a good virus. I'm glad, at least, you are my friend, Arthur."

"Me too," Arthur replies without looking Patty in the eye. "Say, I'm having a birthday party tomorrow. Would you like to come?"

"I'd love to go, but your friends—what will they think?"

"My true friends will like you as much as I like you."

"Arthur, I think that's the sweetest thing anyone has ever said to me."

Arthur blushes.

Patty and Arthur take the rest of the math period to set Patty up in class. But they manage to finish in plenty of time for recess. Except for Arthur and his friends, everyone taunts Patty throughout recess. Arthur knows the teasing isn't because Patty is the new kid in class. Patty scares her classmates to death! The bell rings, ending recess. As Arthur rushes to Patty's side, the teasing and jeering stops.

"I've been insulted before, but it's getting to be a little wearying!" Patty exclaims.

"Patty, I need to let you in on a little secret. When Pembroke was a puppy, the Parvovirus attacked his heart muscles and he almost died. With Pembroke's death our world would have come to an end."

"Your friends think I'm like the deadly Parvovirus and will kill them," replies Patty.

"I'm afraid so."

"I understand, Arthur," Patty consoles her new friend, "Don't worry. Evidently, most bacteria around here haven't seen a good virus. My only hope is that when they get to know me and find out I'm a good virus, they will like me."

Every word Patty says makes sense to Arthur. No one has ever seen a good virus in Pembroke. Arthur decides to trust Patty and hopes things will work out for the best.

Once everyone is seated in class after morning recess, the teacher begins.

"Boys and girls," Mrs. Lactose addresses her students, "on your desk you will find a coin, a die, or a jack with each pointed end of the jack painted blue, green, red, or yellow. Flip the coin or roll the die or spin the jack one hundred times and keep track of the outcomes."

"Teacher, I don't feel so good. May I go to the bathroom?" says Sarah, a girl whose gut is beginning to be upset by the thought of doing mathematics.

"Yes, you may take a hall pass."

"Thank you." Sarah leaves, and the teacher turns her attention back to her students.

"Yes, Patty?" Mrs. Lactose says after seeing Patty's hand raised.

"If we spun our jacks one hundred times and the points came up blue and green twenty-three percent of the time, green and red twenty-five percent of the time, red and yellow twenty-four percent of the time, and yellow and blue twenty-eight percent of the time, do you want us to show our answers in writing or use a graph or show our answers both ways?"

Patty's question stuns the class. Patty is no dummy. The students look back to Mrs. Lactose for her response.

"Excellent question, Patty. I want your answers to be clear and complete. Class," Mrs. Lactose continues, "present your answers in writing and in a graph like Patty suggests. You'll have until the bell for lunch recess sounds to complete your assignment. You may begin."

Patty turns toward Arthur and smiles. She captures a mental picture of him looking at her, as the thought passes through her mind that the differences between their two worlds may never allow them to be friends.

Chapter 2

LUNCH RECESS

PEPSIN ACADEMY'S lunchroom is a large outside area that runs along the last bend of the Great Brown River before it exits through South Port. Arthur takes Patty to the place where he and his friends meet every day to play and eat lunch.

"What do you think, Patty?"

"This is a beautiful spot to have lunch. What's going on across the river?"

"Oh, that—that's Cameron Salt Plant. It's one of last places where salt, some vitamins, and water are taken from the food Pembroke eats."

"This is the last stop where Pembroke's food is processed?"

"Yes. Most of the food nutrients have been digested

in the mouth, stomach, and small intestines, however," Arthur explains.

"You are so smart, Arthur."

Arthur turns red and feels a little uncomfortable, but in a good way.

"I know a lot about this area," he agrees. "But I haven't visited any of Pembroke's other parts. All I know, I've learned through books. I've never traveled any farther than Pembroke's transverse colon."

"Maybe someday, Arthur, we can explore the upper regions of the digestive system together and more!"

Wow! Arthur thinks. *If Patty and I go on up the whole digestive system, what a blast that will be! But what does she mean by "and more"?*

"How old are you going to be on your birthday, Arthur?"

Before Arthur has a chance to answer Patty, his bacteria friends run into the clearing, yelling and laughing. They sit in their usual spots and begin eating and talking. Before long, Patty's question is completely forgotten as the conversations roll on.

"What's your mother packed for you to eat?" Biff asks Amy.

"Yummy things!" Amy says. "I have vitamins B1, B2, B3, B5, and B11. And they taste so good because they come from cocoa and dark chocolate! Mom says the vitamins are good for my skin."

"Who fed Pembroke chocolate? Won't that give him

diarrhea and wipe us out South Port into the Great Expanse?" asks Polly.

"Maybe someone accidentally dropped a chocolate bar and Pembroke found it and ate it," Biff guesses.

Arthur is so alarmed at the possibility of Pembroke eating chocolate that he completely forgets Patty's question about his age. Instead, he jumps into the conversation with his friends.

"No matter how Pembroke got the chocolate, it's a very dangerous thing for him. Diarrhea is no laughing matter down here!"

"I know," Biff agrees. "Well, my mom gave me a wholesome beef and brown rice entrée. She says it will help me be big and strong."

"Pembroke can handle that better," Arthur comments.

"What do you have for lunch?" Ace asks.

"The same thing I have every day—little undigested bits of lamb and beef, some carrots and peas, and part of an apple," Arthur replies.

"Oh, that's good for you, Arthur—a balanced meal," Polly says as she sits down by her best friend, Amy, "My mom gave me some blackberries and dates. She says they will help me to absorb my nutrients and minerals better."

"Your mom is so thoughtful; that sounds so good and healthy for you," Amy says.

Al, Sal, and Casey sit by the edge of the river,

which only flows toward South Port with the help of Pembroke's muscles. They like being together for lunch to share their conversations in private. And, after a few minutes, they will join the others.

"What do you have to eat, Patty?" Amy asks.

"I'm not really hungry."

"I don't mind sharing my lunch with you," Arthur offers.

"You are so thoughtful, Arthur. I'm not hungry because I don't have a stomach," Patty says.

"What?" Arthur reacts.

"I don't have a stomach," Patty repeats. "I know it sound strange; yet, here I am alive and well. And I'm happy to be here sharing lunchtime with you and your friends."

"I still don't get it, Patty!"

"I'm not a bacteria; I'm a virus. I don't have a stomach or a way to digest or get energy from food."

"Then how do you eat? How do you stay alive?" Arthur asks, his curiosity running wild.

"Some human scientists don't believe I am alive. But I get around quite well. I travel in the air, in the water, in the food, and in the blood of animals. As for eating and digesting, I infect living cells and use their digestive systems to eat and digest food for my energy."

The idea that Patty infects living cells and quoted "human scientists" goes right over Arthur's head, because the ideas are not of his world. In Arthur's world, bacteria continuously take in minerals and nutrients, are alive, and reproduce by dividing in half every twenty minutes or so.

"Don't worry, Arthur; I'm alive now. But I can lie dormant for years, decades, or even centuries. We viruses are a different life-form than you are. But it works for us!"

"That's good," Arthur responds, still not quite certain of what Patty is or what she is saying.

"I'm going to let you in on a little inside information, Arthur. I am a DNA molecule wrapped in a protein coat—simple and effective. That's all there is to me."

"Ooookaaaay," Arthur says, quite unsure of himself. Then he asks, "But how do you eat, and where do you get your energy?"

"I infect sick cells and bad bacteria. I use their stomachs to digest food and get what I need. I use the cells I infect to reproduce my kind."

"What happens to those cells and bacteria after you use them?"

"They usually die, but not always."

"You could infect me! And, and use me for your purpose! And kill me!" Arthur says, quite distressed.

"I could, but I won't. You and your friends are good bacteria. I only infect bad cells and bad bacteria and bad viruses. If you and your friends were bad bacteria, I would have infected all of you and reproduced billions of my kind. There would be more of me around here than you could shake a stick at. This school, the playground, the river, and the salt plant across the river would be covered a half of an inch deep with my children."

"Impressive," Arthur whispers, appearing quite distraught.

Overhearing Patty's conversation, Al, Sal, and Casey are terrified. They keep their eyes glued to Patty. They find the thought perplexing that Patty can't reproduce on her own like bacteria do, but can reproduce faster than bacteria by infecting anything she wants. They lean toward Patty and Arthur to hear more.

"How do I know you're really a good virus?" Arthur asks.

"If I was a bad virus—like the West Nile virus or the swine or bird flu viruses—you and your friends would be dead and passed out South Port into the Great Expanse by now."

Arthur is stunned by Patty's revelation. Silence spreads throughout the lunch area, as all of Arthur's friends hear Patty's words. Since they were little, everyone in Pembroke has heard the awful stories about deadly viruses. And although there have been stories of bacteria returning, no one Arthur knows has ever come back after going into the Great Expanse!

"How can we tell the difference between good and bad viruses?" Ace asks.

"If the virus is bad, you're dead. If the virus is good, you're alive."

Another long period of silence sets in at the grove by the river, while Arthur and his friends think long and hard about what Patty is saying.

Cutting through the dark cloud of doom beginning to hang over the grove, Amy shouts, "Does anyone want to play dodge ball?"

"How about a game of tag?" Polly timidly suggests.

Al jumps up and yells, "First one over to the baseball diamond gets first ups!"

Everyone runs like demons to the baseball field.

Leading the way is Al yelling, "I have first ups, I have first ups!"

Everyone jumps up and runs, that is, everyone except for Arthur and Patty, who stay by the river looking at each other.

"Are you really a killer, Patty?"

"Yes, and so we all are to some extent, Arthur. We all live by ingesting plants and animals for food, unless we simply suck minerals from rocks."

"I guess so. I never really looked at it that way before. You're right. Bacteria can infect living things too. But the bacteria living in Southern Pembroke are good bacteria and only serve to help Pembroke."

"You're not that different from me, Arthur."

"Maybe so."

The bell ending recess sounds. Patty and Arthur are

in no hurry to be first in line. By the time they enter the classroom, everyone has heard rumors about what Patty said at lunch. Classmates move out of Patty's way as she goes to her desk.

"Like Moses parting the sea," one bacterium classmate is heard saying.

Chapter 3

BIRTHDAY BOY

PATTY WATCHES her parents take the seven fifteen morning sneeze out of Portsmouth to parts unknown in the Great Expanse. For a while, she observes the dust and pollen and germs enter Pembroke's nose from the Great Expanse and watches large water molecules leave from Pembroke's lungs and out his mouth into the Great Expanse. In time Patty leaves to find her way back to Southern Pembroke for Arthur's birthday party. She catches the first doggie treat bound south and transfers at Belly Station, taking the Brighter Maroon River Express to Rectum Hall. On the station platform she sets her direction for Arthur's house. She rolls from the train station up Canal Street and turns on Grove Street, where Louie, Honey, and Arthur live in an exclusive colony of floral bacteria. Finding 1727 Grove Street, Patty rings the doorbell.

"You must be Patty. Arthur's told us all about you," a tall, friendly honey-colored bacterium warmly welcomes her. "I'm Arthur's mother. Please come in. Arthur is so excited that you are coming to his birthday party. Would you like anything to eat?"

"No thank you, Mrs. Bacterium," Patty says. "I'm not hungry. Maybe later."

Honey Bacterium smiles and escorts Patty to the family room. She calls for the birthday boy to come out and greet his guest.

"Arthur, Patty's here to play with you."

Arthur appears at the top of the stairs. "Can Patty come up here and play, Mother?"

"Sure, dear. Are you dressed and ready to go to your birthday party?"

"Yes, Mom. I'm ready."

Patty, in all of her orangeness, floats up the spiral staircase on her feathery spikes to the second floor, where Arthur takes her to his playroom.

"You have a lot of toys to play with, Arthur."

"Mostly bits and pieces of enzymes. Here's my favorite game, Patty," he says while showing her the game box.

"'Surgery'?" Patty reads the name on the box. "How do we play Surgery, Arthur?"

Arthur opens the box, which reveals a large plastic

cat lying on its back. He takes his tweezers and opens the flaps over the cat's torso.

"You take your tweezers and try to remove the cat's body parts without touching the cat's body. If you touch the body, a buzzer goes off and the other person gets a chance to do cat surgery."

"That sounds like fun. You go first."

Arthur tries to remove the kidney. *Buzz!*

"Your turn, Patty. I messed up."

"Why did you start with the kidney, Arthur? That's hard to remove because it's so close to the stomach and liver. I bet you don't even know what the kidney does."

"Yes, I do," insists Arthur. "The kidney gets rid of some of the waste and junk Pembroke eats."

"Very good; you're right. Smart boy."

Arthur is so happy he impressed Patty. He wanted to impress her in the first place when he tried and failed to remove the kidney.

"Your turn, Patty. What are you going to remove?"

"I'm going to remove the heart."

Patty successfully removes the heart and holds it in the air.

"It looks like a large muscle," Arthur observes.

"Yes," replies Patty. "And do you know what the heart does?"

Arthur is stumped. He knows the digestive system well—the colon, intestines, gallbladder, pancreas, liver, stomach, esophagus, salivary glands, and mouth—but the heart is part of Pembroke's circulatory system, which Arthur doesn't know much about. Patty does not want to embarrass her new friend in his own house and does not press Arthur to tell her what the heart does. Rather, she very carefully answers her own question in a way to protect Arthur's feelings.

"I may be wrong, but I think the heart pumps blood all around Pembroke."

Arthur is quick to answer, "Yes, Patty. I think you are right."

Their conversation is interrupted by a call from downstairs, "Arthur? Patty? Dad and I are ready to go to the birthday party."

Arthur replies immediately to his mother, "Okay, we're on our way."

Patty and Arthur run down the stairs and meet Arthur's parents outside the front door.

"So you're Patty," says Louie, who is Arthur's dad.

"I'm Patty Virus, Mr. Bacterium," she replies.

"I've heard a lot of good things about you."

"Like what?" Patty responds with all of her eyes wide open.

Louie laughs as they head out to Grove Street.

"Well, like how smart you are, Patty. And I've heard how nice you are. And even better, I heard that you didn't infect Arthur and his friends at school yesterday!"

Everyone laughs as they turn up Canal Street

toward Houston Park, where Arthur's birthday party will be held way above the Great Brown River. With his mother by his side, Arthur leads the family up the side of rectum wall. Patty remains back to talk with Louie.

"Patty, may I ask where you come from?"

"Sure, Mr. Bacterium. I was floating in the air with my family when I was breathed in by Pembroke."

"Where did you stay last night?"

"I was with my parents at the Airport Inn in Portsmouth. When they flew out of Pembroke this morning, I came back to South Pembroke."

"So, you're here alone?"

"Yes, I'm all alone, but that's how I like to travel around the world."

"I find that amazing," Louie admits as if he discovered something new. "Do you mind my asking you how got here so fast from the airport?"

"Not at all. I took the Brighter Maroon River Express."

Looking very surprised, Louie says, "You weren't stopped by the organ police or the reserves?"

"Should I have been stopped by the police?"

"You know, Patty, Pembroke is a very secure place to live—if you stay in the digestive system. But if you travel in Pembroke's circulatory system or nervous system or any other system outside of his digestive system, Pembroke's police should have eliminated you!"

"What do you mean?"

"You see this rectum wall we're climbing?"

"Yes."

"The wall is thick and is constantly watched by the police to prevent really bad stuff from getting out of Pembroke's digestive system and into other parts of his body," Louie comments.

"Does that include us? Are we considered bad stuff, Mr. Bacterium?"

"Absolutely," Louie responds. "But it's up to the police and reserves to decide. If lots of bacteria or viruses grow and pose a threat to Pembroke, the police and reserves will attack and kill them!"

"I don't like traveling with a bunch a viruses. They attract too much attention from immune systems. That's one of two reasons why I like traveling alone," Patty responds.

Hmm, Louie says to himself, *I wonder what Patty's other reason is for wanting to travel alone?*

Louie and Patty reach Houston Park around one o'clock in the afternoon and sit at the party table with Honey, Arthur, and millions of Arthur's aunts, uncles, cousins, and friends. Over five hundred thousand bacteria from Grove Street are at Arthur's party too, which makes Arthur a very happy birthday boy. They drink water, eat a little salt, laugh, and joke around.

"Geronimo!" shouts Ace, a red sphere, as he takes off from the diving board.

Everyone watches Ace float into the river and climb back up the wall to the park.

"Come on guys, Bacteria unite!" Ace calls to Arthur and the rest of the gang. "Let's fly away."

"Do you want to jump, Patty?"

"No, I'll stay here and talk with your parents. But go ahead, have fun, birthday boy."

Being older than Arthur and his friends and being in a new environment, Patty prefers to hang out with the adult bacteria and find out what they think and how they relate to her.

"Geronimo! Geronimo!" Arthur and Ace shout as they dive off the board hand in hand.

"Geronimo!" Al, a green spherical bacterium; Sal, a green rod-shaped bacterium; and Casey, a blue spherical-shaped bacterium shout, as they run together on the diving board, bounce, and fly into space.

The river is refreshing and lots of fun. Soon rods and spherical bacteria of all colors are jumping from the diving board at Houston Park into the river far below. In time, everyone at the party has taken a dive off the board—even Patty, Honey, and Louie. Afterward, Honey calls everyone to the table to sing "Happy Birthday" to Arthur.

"What kind of birthday cake is it, Mrs. Bacterium?" asks Casey.

"Oh, it's a very delicious and nutritious carrot cake with vanilla yogurt frosting," Honey answers.

Turning around, Honey asks Louie to do the honors. Louie takes matches out of his pocket and strikes one. As everyone's gaze follows Louie's hand, he lights the first candle on the cake and phosphorous smoke fills the air. When the candle ignites and sparks fly about, the younger bacteria "ooh" and "aah." Soon all nine candles are lit and sparks are flying all around the table.

Rapidly Arthur climbs up on a chair, smiles at his millions of friends and relatives, and makes a wish. He blows as hard as he can. All but one candle goes out. Standing tall in the carrot cake, with its flame still burning in the smoke, the last candle waits for the final blow, which Arthur delivers quickly. The flame is extinguished, and cheers and applause fill Rectum Hall. Arthur cuts the cake, while Honey and Patty serve the guests.

"I feel warm in here," Patty whispers to Louie.

"That's okay, Patty. When Pembroke releases this smoke and hot air through South Port, I'm sure we'll catch a breeze. Things will be just fine," Louie assures her.

Patty asks, "Where are Arthur's presents?"

"Oh, that's right. This is the first bacteria birthday party you've been to," Honey replies.

Patty nods.

"Everyone that comes to a bacteria birthday party is a birthday present. The gift of family and friends being together is highly valued in bacteria colonies."

Patty is delighted with Mrs. Bacterium's answer. She never thought about it that way before. Mrs. Bacterium is right. We are great gifts to each other.

When it is time to go home, everyone hugs each other good-bye. Arthur—the birthday boy—and Honey, Louie, and Patty are given special hugs because the partygoers love and appreciate Arthur and his family.

Patty feels loved. She has never been hugged by so many bacteria before. Everyone is usually so afraid of being killed that they either try to kill her or fly in terror away from her. She is so happy that she forgets how different she is from all the bacteria in Pembroke.

After the party, Honey asks, "Patty, would you like to stay over at our house tonight? Mr. Bacterium, Arthur, and I would be so happy to have your company. I know Arthur would be especially happy with the gift of your presence in our home."

"Why, yes, Mrs. Bacterium. I'd like that," says a thrilled Patty. "I'd like that very much."

On the way home, Louie and Arthur lead the way, while Patty and Honey stay back and talk.

"Patty, I've watched you and Arthur play, and I see how much Arthur likes you. Do you like Arthur?" Honey asks.

"I do like Arthur. He's my best friend, Mrs. Bacterium. Is that alright?"

"You wanting him as your best friend is perfectly fine with me, Patty."

"Do you mind that I'm a virus?"

"I don't mind that you're a virus. I have never met a virus like you before. All I wanted to know was if you were going to harm Arthur someday."

"Harm Arthur! No—I would never hurt Arthur. I do understand your fear, Mrs. Bacterium. I don't blame you for wanting to protect your boy. I want to protect him too."

"That's good to know, Patty," Honey confides.

By the time everyone reaches home, Honey and Patty have formed a close bond.

"Patty, I would love for you to call me Honey instead of Mrs. Bacterium. I feel like you're one of the family."

Patty averts her eyes to the river and says, "Thank you, Honey. Outside of my species, that's the nicest anyone has every treated me. I love being part of your family."

That evening, Patty watches the Bacterium family enjoy dinner. Afterward, Arthur and Patty play in his room until bedtime. Arthur shows Patty to the guest bedroom and gives her a big hug. They smile.

"I had a wonderful time at your birthday party, Arthur. I've never felt so loved in my whole life," Patty says with tears forming in her eyes.

"It is the best birthday party I've ever had, Patty. Thank you for being here."

"Good night, Mr. Bacterium. Good night, Honey," Patty calls from her bedroom.

Louie bids good night to Patty.

"Good night, Mom and Dad," calls Arthur.

"Good night, Arthur," his dad replies.

Honey climbs the stairs. She will say her good nights after tucking Arthur in bed and visiting Patty to tuck her in bed too.

Chapter 4

PROFESSOR AND THE VIRUS

EARLY THE next morning, Patty wakes first and quietly goes downstairs, trying not to rouse the Bacteria family. She walks into the kitchen and finds Louie having coffee.

"Good morning, Patty. I'd offer you cereal, but I know you don't need to eat like we do."

"Kind of you to think of me. You do know a lot about viruses, don't you?"

"Quite a bit. I'm a professor of virology at Der Kot University."

"Do you know about my family, Professor?"

"Not unless you tell me where your family is from. I don't want to nose around in your private life."

"You've been very kind to me and treated me like

one of your family. That goes a long way, Professor. Besides, you could have more to fear from me than I have to fear from you."

"That's the truth. I am curious why you haven't infected any of us."

"I'm one of the Nelson Viruses."

"Admiral Lord Nelson?"

"Yes," Patty answers, seeing a gleam come to the professor's eyes.

"I know the history of the Nelson Virus well. No wonder you didn't infect us. You're from a very good orange strain of viruses."

Beaming, Patty says, "Yes. I'm no threat to you or Pembroke. Tell me more about what you know about my ancestors."

"Here's my favorite story. You know Admiral Nelson died at the Battle of Trafalgar. It was his best victory, but alas, his final day on earth. When he passed away, he was put in a barrel of brandy alcohol mixed with camphor and myrrh to preserve his body for the long trip back to London. At his funeral, he was placed in a lead-lined coffin filled with spirits of wine."

"Wouldn't all that alcohol kill the bacteria and viruses in his body, Professor?"

"Exactly. All of the bacteria in Nelson's body that were immersed in the drinking alcohol died. But some of the viruses survived. It seems your ancestors survived and adapted well to the brandy and formed a new strain of virus."

"Wow! Think of that, Pro—do you mind if I call you Professor, Mr. Bacterium?"

"If you want to call me Professor, that's alright with me."

Patty is so excited to find out more from the professor about her family than she has ever known before that she almost pops with joy.

"Yes," the professor continues. "Your family may have left Pembroke by air yesterday morning, but their favorite way to travel is by sea."

"That's why I always liked the water," Patty says. "I love the oceans, lakes, and rivers—anything wet."

"Seventy-five to eighty percent of Pembroke is water," the professor explains. "That's why you travel so well throughout Pembroke."

Patty listens to the professor and learns. She trusts this large spherical blue bacterium with the bright blue mustache and bright blue beard and broad friendly smile.

"Professor, remember how you were surprised that I could take the Brighter Maroon River Express without attracting the police or the reserves?"

"Yes."

"And you remember I told you there were two reasons why I'm not afraid to travel alone?"

"I remember and still can't figure out that second reason."

"Over the years Professor, Nelson viruses developed a secret weapon, a cloaking device."

"You mean you've become invisible to the police and the reserves the immune system sends out to kill you?"

"When my family and I entered Pembroke, we cloaked ourselves. Pembroke's immune system couldn't detect us."

"Your cloaking device works well in Pembroke?"

"So far I've been in Pembroke's digestive, circulatory, and respiratory systems and am here to talk about it. The cloaking device works everywhere I've been— dogs, cats, fish, cows, whales, humans, plants, and microorganisms," reveals Patty.

"Amazing! What are dogs, cats, fish, cows, whales, humans, plants, and microorganisms?"

"They're names given to different life-forms that exist in the Great Expanse."

"How wonderful to learn about these things. I know everything there is to know about what's inside of Pembroke. I've heard many stories about the Great Expanse told by bacteria supposedly coming into Pembroke from the Great Expanse, but I have never been outside Pembroke to scientifically prove or disprove their stories."

"Have there been any scientific expeditions into the Great Expanse?"

The professor appears sad.

"Unfortunately not. All our information about the Great Expanse has come from strange bacteria invading Pembroke on dust particles and water molecules through Portsmouth or from bacteria coming back when Pembroke eats dog poop."

"Very limited information about the Great Expanse," Patty comments.

"Someday I hope to lead a scientific expedition into the Great Expanse. My hours are running short, however."

"Don't give up hope on your dream, Professor. I can teach you what I know about the Great Expanse. We can learn from each other."

"Yes, we can learn from each other. And so we will!"

"Professor, about the invisible cloaking device, that must stay our secret. Not even the human scientists know about our cloaking device!"

"Human scientists?" the professor expresses surprise.

"Yes, scientists like you. Except these human scientists believe they are the only and most knowledgeable and most advanced scientists in the Great Expanse, which from their point of view includes Pembroke."

"That's quite a joke! For all their knowledge and

advancement, they have not discovered your viral cloaking device or fellow scientists like me. That's rich! What an arrogant species they must be."

"You don't know the half of it, Professor. The joke is on them. Only Nelson Viruses and you know."

"I won't tell a living soul about your cloaking device. However, I would like to share everything else you tell me about the Great Expanse with my family, friends, and students."

"I know I could count on you. You have my permission to share anything else I tell you about the Great Expanse with anyone you want, Professor."

"Do you mind my asking how old you are?"

"Not at all, but that's a difficult question for me to answer. Compared to Arthur, I'm about five thousand times his age."

"I would have guessed as much. I think you will be good for Arthur. You certainly know your way around the Great Expanse. You are very wise, and you have a cloaking device protecting you. Very interesting," the professor says, stroking his bright blue beard.

"Why do you ask me about my age?"

"I have a secret too, Patty. I probably won't be able to personally study the Great Expanse. But I want Arthur to have a shot at it. I want him to learn and be amazed by everything, especially the world outside of Pembroke's digestive system. And, Patty, I think you two make a good team."

"You want Arthur and me to explore the world outside of Pembroke's digestive system and the Great Expanse?" Patty blurts out.

"That's my hope. But let's start small. Summer vacation begins at the end of next week. That's a great time to explore a couple of systems inside Pembroke."

Patty says, "You want me and Arthur to explore Pembroke, even if we go outside of the digestive system?"

"Yes, Arthur has never gone beyond the transverse colon. Start in the digestive system and see how far you two can go. Take the whole bacteria summer, if you like. That gives you lots of time to travel Pembroke's highways and byways."

"How will your wife feel about this, Professor?"

"Honey and I have discussed Arthur's dream of exploring the digestive system and beyond and the dangers such a journey holds for him. Honey supports the two of you taking the summer to explore what you can."

"And the Great Expanse?"

"I'd like to wait until we see how the jaunt through Pembroke's digestive system and maybe a couple of his other body systems work out before raising Arthur's expectations and Honey's anxieties about exploring the Great Expanse."

"That's a fair deal, Professor," Patty responds.

"I have to admit the possibility of Arthur being

killed scares us, but he's an exceptionally curious boy. More of a scientist than I was at his age."

"If the cloaking device I have can somehow protect Arthur too, Professor, that would solve a lot of problems."

"I've been thinking about that. I believe your cloaking device will work with Arthur. However, we really won't know until you test the device on Arthur outside of the digestive system ..." The professor pauses.

"And that may be too late for Arthur," Patty says, finishing the professor's thought.

"There is the unfortunate possibility that Arthur could lose his life. We can discuss this later, Patty, if you'd like."

"Yes, we'll talk about it later, Professor."

Dressed for work, Honey bounces into the kitchen.

"You two seem to be deep in conversation this morning."

"Good observation, dear. We have been discussing the possibility of Patty taking Arthur on a little summer vacation up Pembroke's digestive system and maybe beyond."

"Exactly what I hoped. I know Arthur would love it. He is quite the little adventurer. Where exactly would they go?"

"I think they could follow the Great Brown River up to Acid Lake for starters, if that's okay with you, Honey," the professor suggests.

"That's fine with me. What about the beyond part?"

Before Patty can answer, a sleepy-eyed Arthur drags himself into the kitchen.

"Why didn't anyone wake me up?" Arthur asks demandingly.

"Looks like someone's grumpy this morning," Honey observes.

"Yes, Mom. I want to be in on the fun, not sleep my life away!"

"Okay," Honey says. "I have a lecture to give on fruit bacteria and need to get going."

"On Sunday, Mom?"

"Yes, on Sunday, dear."

Before bouncing out the door, she kisses the professor, Arthur, and Patty.

"Be sure to feed Arthur a good breakfast, dear," Honey calls back to the professor.

"You can be sure of that, dear." Turning to Arthur, the professor asks, "How about some fermented banana pancakes?"

"That's my favorite, Dad. What else?"

"How would you like to take this summer to explore the digestive system with Patty?"

Arthur looks at Patty. Patty nods and smiles.

"Patty, you said you might take me exploring past the transverse colon and more! You're a girl who keeps her promises. I'd love to go on an adventure with Patty this summer, Dad. Thanks."

"We're only talking about exploring the digestive system for now, son. We'll talk later about what you mean by 'more.'"

"Okay, Dad. That's fine with me. These pancakes really taste great. May I have a glass of salt water too?"

"Of course, son."

While Arthur is concentrating on his breakfast, Patty and the professor slip away through the living room and out onto the patio. Sliding the patio door closed behind them so Arthur can't hear, the professor turns and speaks to Patty in a soft voice.

"Patty, I've given more thought to your cloaking device. I calculate you have enough energy to protect Arthur too."

"That's good news, Professor."

"With protection like that, you and Arthur could travel anywhere you wanted inside of Pembroke."

"You mean, you are giving me permission to travel with Arthur outside of the digestive system?"

"I've been watching you, Patty. You are a very mature and wise virus. Now that I'm sure your cloaking device is powerful enough to protect the both of you, I know you will take good care of Arthur."

"I understand."

"But it's your final call, Patty. If for some reason you don't feel right about going out of the digestive system, don't explore any farther."

"I understand, Professor. It's my call."

Arthur sees his dad and Patty talking and runs through the living room and out to the patio.

"What are you two talking about?"

"It's a surprise," his dad says. "You will find out in due time, Arthur."

"I want to know now, Dad! Quit treating me like a child. Why do I always have to be the last one to know?" Arthur demands.

Arthur's dad takes him into the next room and closes the door.

"I know you want to know what Patty and I were talking about, son. But, it's a surprise. You barged into the conversation I was having with Patty. That was rude of you, son. Just try to be a little more patient."

"Oh, all right, Dad. I'm sorry."

"Apology accepted. Now go in there and entertain Patty before she wonders if she's in trouble too."

"Everything's all right, Patty. Let's go outside and play."

Patty and Arthur dash out of the house and join the neighborhood kids down by the river. Arthur and Patty have so much fun playing hide-and-seek with the neighborhood kids that Arthur forgets about wanting to know what his father and Patty were talking about. When he does remember, he decides not to bring the question up and let whatever happens be the surprise it was meant to be.

Chapter 5

GREAT BROWN RIVER

MONDAY MORNING begins the bacteria children's summer vacation. Preparing to launch their kayak, Arthur and Patty gather with family and friends on the Pepsin Academy playground by the Great Brown River, where Arthur and his friends always eat lunch. A week's food provisions are stored in the bow hatch of Arthur and Patty's kayak. Extra clothing is stored in the stern hatch. The professor and Ace steady the kayak as Patty climbs into the front seat. Arthur sits in the backseat, next to the rudder. Honcy, the Bacterium family, and their friends watch and wave as Patty and Arthur paddle up the Great Brown River on the first leg of their adventure. The professor puts his arm around Honey, giving her a little squeeze as they wave *bon voyage* to their son and Patty. They watch their lavender son and orange Patty fade into the distance.

"We're off, Patty!"

"I'm excited too, Arthur. How far are we from Sigmoid Bend?"

"About a half an hour is my guess."

"What is up there?" Patty asks.

"It's beautiful. Wait and you'll see for yourself."

Patty is motivated to see the big bend and paddles long and strong.

"Look, Arthur, I see a curve up ahead."

"Yep, that's the beginning of the Sigmoid Bend, the only S-curve in the lower colon. I saw it last summer, when we were vacationing. We're making good time. I hope things ahead aren't stopped up."

"Stopped up?" Patty replies.

"Yeah, if Pembroke eats lots of fatty meats, cheese, and junk food, then the waste gets all hard, making it impossible to paddle our kayak through. We will have to carry our kayak over land."

"That doesn't sound like fun."

"Believe me, it isn't fun; it's hard work. And Pembroke may have to be operated on to remove the stopped-up waste in his colon."

"That's not good."

"No. It's not good at all. If Pembroke is stopped up real bad, he could die," Arthur continues.

"Die?"

"If Pembroke gets constipated for a long period of time and can't digest his food, poisons build up that can kill him. With everything stopped up, he could even starve to death."

"I hope Pembroke is eating the right foods," Patty replies.

"Me too. If he doesn't, those smooth muscles you see around the walls of the colon won't move the waste down the river and out South Port."

"That would be terrible, Arthur!"

"We'd have to walk all the way back home—and that's a long walk."

However, good news is around the bend. Pembroke has been eating lots of vegetables, fruits, cereals, and lean meats. The paddling is just fine. Instead of it being dark and gloomy kayaking up the Great Brown River, the earth's sun beats down on Pembroke, lighting up the inside of his colon. Shining through the hundreds of thousands of blood capillaries inside the colon walls, the sun creates hues of ruby, pink, and rose for the two travelers to enjoy.

"You weren't kidding, Arthur. This is beautiful country and the reddish tones radiating through Pembroke reminds me of being in a church with large stained glass windows."

Patty puts on her sunglasses.

"A church?" Arthur says, puzzled.

"That's right—you've never been outside of

Pembroke, have you, Arthur? A church is a place where people go to worship God."

"People? God? Worship? I don't get it. I've heard sounds from outside of Pembroke and have been tossed around when he moves about, but I've never been outside. What's it like?"

"Oh, the stories I could tell you, Arthur. But I'll save them for later. What are those towns along the walls?"

"From here to the transverse colon, we'll be seeing nothing but small colonies of floral bacteria that help Pembroke digest his food."

"All those good vitamins, minerals, proteins, and sugars from the food Pembroke eats are distributed from here to all parts of Pembroke?" Patty reasons.

"No, all that's left here are salts and water for Pembroke. Digestion of most of that good stuff you mentioned takes place in the small intestines."

"What happens if Pembroke eats bad foods?"

"Good question. If Pembroke eats bad foods, then the blood vessels will transport poisons and toxins to all parts of his body too."

"That's not good," Patty says.

"Not good at all! If Pembroke eats good foods, he should live for fifteen, even twenty healthy years— maybe more. With bad foods he will get fat, have a bad back, and have internal problems. He will develop cancers, and he will go blind faster. He may only live nine or ten years or less."

"Let's not think of that right now and keep paddling and enjoying ourselves."

Arthur paddles for hours through the sigmoid, up the descending colon. By the time they round Spleen Turn and beach their kayak at Hepatic Mountain Bend, Arthur is seventeen hours old.

"Are you having a happy birthday, Arthur?"

"This is the first time I've had birthdays without my family and friends. I thought I would miss having birthday parties, but I love celebrating with you, Patty. This is as far as I've ever been inside Pembroke!"

"Congratulations, Arthur. Hepatic Mountain Bend looks like a great place to have a picnic birthday party," suggests Patty.

"Good idea. I'm famished," Arthur says, looking at his watch. "We are averaging about an inch an hour—pretty good time!"

Ever mindful of Pembroke's natural environment, Honey packed only the healthiest foods for the trip. Everything that goes into the Great Brown River will be absorbed into Pembroke's bloodstream. Patty and Arthur are careful not to pollute.

"Patty?"

"Yes."

"You said you would tell me stories about being

outside of Pembroke. How about telling me a story now?"

"The world outside of Pembroke. Hum. Well, the outside world is filled with air. You wouldn't be living in dog poop."

"Oh, how strange. What's air?"

"You know how sometimes gas forms in Pembroke? Air is like that gas, except it doesn't smell funny."

"Pembroke's gas doesn't smell funny! What do you mean by that?" Arthur protests.

"That's right—you are used to Pembroke's gas. The air outside is made of oxygen and hydrogen and nitrogen and would have no smell."

"Interesting," responds Arthur.

"You know that red light shining through Pembroke?"

"Yes."

"That comes from the sun," Patty explains.

Arthur asks a ton of questions about the sun and the world outside of Pembroke. Patty does her best to answer all of Arthur's questions. Seconds go buy as the two have lunch and discuss worlds beyond Pembroke that Arthur has never dreamed about. He takes in everything Patty tells him like a dry sponge thrown in the ocean. After a great lunch of carrots, oats, and blackberries, Arthur paddles down the ascending colon, arriving at Cecum Hollow on schedule. They tie the kayak near the end of the Hollow, exactly where the small intestine begins. Arthur can't stop asking questions. Patty has no trouble answering all of his questions because she has traveled the Great Expanse for more than five human years.

It's peaceful in the Hollow, and the two have no trouble resting. Tired by their long journey, the big meal, and the minutes of discussion, they manage to sleep soundly. Not even Pembroke's snoring and the rubbing noises from Pembroke's stomach, small intestines, and colon muscles constantly moving keep Patty and Arthur awake. They sleep through the bacteria night and wake the next morning rested and refreshed.

"What do we have before us today, Arthur?" Patty asks.

"About a foot or so of twists and turns through the small intestines before we reach the spot where chyme and chemicals are poured into the upper part of the small intestines," Arthur replies.

"Chyme? Chemicals?" responds Patty.

"The food Pembroke eats is mixed with saliva and goes into his stomach where hydrochloric acid makes the food into a soft paste, called chyme. The chyme moves into the beginning of the small intestine where liver, pancreas, and gallbladder bile also flow into the intestine, mix with the chyme, and further dissolves Pembroke's food so it can go into his bloodstream."

"What does all that liver, pancreas, and gallbladder bile do?"

"The liver and pancreatic bile dissolves or breaks-down carbohydrates, fats, and proteins in the food. The bile from the gallbladder helps Pembroke absorb vitamins into his bloodstream."

"Lots of chemicals helping Pembroke digest his food," Patty comments.

"It's all done automatically. Pembroke doesn't feel anything happening, unless something goes wrong. And that's not all. You notice all the little fingerlike projections hanging from the walls of the intestines?"

Patty looks into the small intestines and says, "Yes."

"Well," continues Arthur, who is sounding more and more like his dad, the professor, "Those are called villi. If you look real close you will see little things hanging from the villi, called microvilli. That's where the sugars, proteins, carbohydrates, and vitamins and minerals from the digested food go into the bloodstream so they can be taken to all parts of Pembroke."

"Interesting. Won't all these chemicals hurt us, Arthur?"

"There are bacteria that live and do well in the small intestines, Patty. But the acids and chemicals are not that strong in and around South Pembroke, where I live. I don't know exactly how the acids and chemicals will affect us. Maybe, we'll get a little burned."

"Like a suntan?" Patty responds.

"What's a suntan?" Arthur replies.

"Oh, I'll tell you later about suntans. I guess a little acid burn won't hurt," Patty says, ready to accept the risk. "I have a swim suit. Let's get started."

After several hours more of travel, they pass by a large bacteria colony that leads to a dead end.

"What's that huge cave we just passed?" Patty asks.

"That's the appendix. A lot of bacteria live in colonies there. My cousin Steve lives in one of the colonies. And that's where my mom was born."

"Honey was born there?'

"Yes."

"Do you want to go back and visit Steve?"

"Maybe next trip. I'm too eager to head farther up the river to the stomach. I hear Acid Lake is beautiful this time of year."

"Let's go," Patty says enthusiastically.

Patty and Arthur continue to paddle their kayak up the Great Brown River. The farther they get up river, the more tanned they get, because the acids and bile in the river are getting stronger. After hours of paddling, they reach Twelve Fingers. Paddling a little farther, they arrive at the Sphincter of Oddi. Faintly, in the distance, around Duodenal Curve, they hear the chyme roaring out of the stomach.

"We have a decision to make, Arthur," Patty says, looking Arthur right in the eyes. "It's a life and death decision for you, my friend!"

Arthur stops breathing.

He can hardly talk, but he manages to ask Patty in a shaky, thin voice, "What do you mean by a life or death decision, Patty?"

Chapter 6

HEPATIC MOUNTAIN

ARTHUR WAITS a long time for Patty to answer.

"I'm afraid we have reached the end of our journey, unless …"

"Unless what?" Arthur warily replies.

"Unless you want to leave the digestive system and explore some of Pembroke's other systems."

Arthur knows that if he leaves the digestive system, he risks being attacked by agents of Pembroke's immune system—the organ police and T cells and antibodies and NK cells and white cells. Arthur worries about being hunted down and killed.

"I guess that ends our vacation. At least I got past the transverse colon."

"As I see it, we have several options," Patty says not losing eye contact with Arthur. "First, as you say, we can turn around and go back to Southern Pembroke. Second, we can continue paddling along Twelve Fingers through the pyloric sphincter into Acid Lake, exit from the stomach, and travel up the esophagus to Pembroke's mouth, which completes our trip through the digestive system. Third, we can paddle through the microvilli and enter Pembroke's bloodstream. Or—"

"Or what?" Arthur responds full of anticipation.

"Or we can paddle through the Sphincter of Oddi and travel through the common bile duct past the gall bladder and pancreas to Hepatic Mountain. Each journey presents grave danger for you, Arthur."

"I'm more worried about your safety than mine, Patty. You may be killed by agents from Pembroke's immune system."

"I have a protective cloaking device that makes me invisible to agents sent by Pembroke's immune system. I'll be safe; but you don't have any protection at all."

"That's so cool. I wish I had a cloaking device that made me invisible."

"I talked to your dad, and he thinks I can protect you as well as protect myself."

"How is that going to work?"

"We need to become one, you and I."

"Oh, like symbiosis," Arthur says.

"No, more like I'll attach myself to your back like a parasite."

"But parasites attach themselves to the surface of

a cell wall and stick things inside of them. Won't that kill me?"

"Parasites do not kill their hosts, Arthur. They want their hosts to stay alive and well."

"I've read that some parasites do kill their hosts. I'm afraid, Patty!"

"I won't let that happen to you, Arthur. I like you a lot, and I promised your parents I would bring you home safely. I will attach myself to your back without hurting you. You may feel a little bunch of pinches from my feathery attachments, but you will not be harmed. This is the only way I can share my invisibility shield with you."

"Sweet!" Arthur says excitedly, still not fully understanding. "What are we waiting for? Let's do it!" he says, throwing caution to the wind.

Arthur stands in the kayak and steadies himself by holding on to one of the microvilli protruding from the intestine wall. Patty climbs the length of Arthur's tall lavender body and settles in on his back. Arthur feels like a small child is playing piggyback with him. Patty's and Arthur's large, inquisitive eyes innocently peer into the unknown before they gradually disappear from sight. Arthur carefully sits down in the kayak. He takes hold of the paddle.

"I can't see my hands and feet. I'm invisible. Wow!"

"Can you see me, Arthur?"

"No, I can't see you, anywhere."

"Can you feel where I am?" Patty asks as she snuggles in closer on his back, placing her orange feathery spikes into his back.

"Yes, I feel you, Patty."

"Good, we are connected. Everything I see, you see. Everything I sense, you sense."

"This is so cool. Wow! What a trip!"

"This is new for me too. Your job is to both steer and paddle the kayak. We'll have to coordinate our thoughts and movements without seeing each other. Try picking up the paddle."

"I already have the paddle," Arthur announces as he uses it to hold the kayak in place against the river current.

"And the rudder?" Patty asks.

"The rudder is firmly tied in place. From here on out, I'll use only the paddle to do all of the steering and supply all the power for our trip," Arthur replies.

"Good. Now that we are protected from Pembroke's immune system, what do you want to do? Go through the pyloric sphincter into the stomach and on to the mouth? Take the Sphincter of Oddi up the pancreatic duct to the Hepatic Mountain? Enter Pembroke's bloodstream through one of those microvilli hanging around us?"

"Let's start paddling toward the Sphincter of Oddi," Arthur responds, maneuvering the kayak close to Oddi.

"Okay, Arthur," Patty says. "When you see some green goo coming out of that hole in the wall, paddle like our lives depend on it, because if we don't get past the sphincter muscle and it closes on us, we're goners."

Arthur and Patty patiently wait for the moment Patty described.

"The Sphincter of Oddi is beginning to relax," Patty says.

Arthur paddles as fast as he can into the flow of goo coming from Oddi. Halfway through the sphincter, he looks up as it begins to close. He paddles faster. Patty closes her eyes, waiting for the worst to happen, as they attempt to zoom into the bile duct.

"*Scrunch!*" the Sphincter of Oddi sounds as it squeezes shut behind them.

"No sweat," Arthur says, "We made it through with microinches to spare."

In a moment of glee, Arthur forgets he is out of the digestive system and subject to attack by Pembroke's immune system. Patty keeps a lookout for Pembroke's killer and white cells, but so far her protective shield seems to be working.

"Paddle the kayak to the left, or we will go through the duct leading into the pancreas," Patty directs.

Arthur paddles left as Patty says, and they safely pass the pancreatic duct.

"Where are we?" Arthur asks.

"We are in the common bile duct, the passageway that carries different kinds of bile made by the pancreas we passed on our right, the gallbladder ahead on our left, and the Hepatic Mountain straight ahead. Steer carefully and paddle slowly," Patty orders.

"All this bile goes in Twelve Fingers to digest Pembroke's food?"

"Yes, sirree. Keep to the right or we will go up the wrong duct to the gallbladder."

Arthur alertly follows Patty's command and stays clear of the cystic duct, which goes to the gallbladder.

"Excellent," Patty compliments Arthur. "Hold steady and keep going straight."

Arthur is a good navigator and exactly follows Patty's commands.

"Ahead of us lays the large reddish-brown Hepatic Mountain, looming as high as the eye can see. But we can't see it from here inside the common duct. When we get inside of the mountain, things will open up a lot!" Patty comments.

Arthur paddles from the duct to the inside the mountain. Gawking upward at the inside of Hepatic Mountain, Arthur is amazed. Hundreds and hundreds of small globs—each having arteries and veins attached—spread out as far as the eye can see.

"Oh my!" exclaims Arthur, "I've never seen anything like this before. What are those things?"

"Filters. Hepatic Mountain is a huge filtering system

that cleans up the blood plasma in Pembroke's body. It purifies the blood by taking out poisons and wastes of all kinds."

"It looks like a huge tree with hundreds of thousands of tiny leaves," continues Arthur, still full of wonder.

"Great description, Arthur. Ninety-eight percent of the fatty foods, pesticides, and other stuff Pembroke eats, as well as the airborne chemicals he breathes and the old, dead, and broken cells in his bloodstream are cleaned up in the Hepatic Mountain. Pembroke needs all of those hundreds of thousands of filters to do the job. While he does get a little help from his kidneys and lymphatic systems, pancreas, and gall bladder, the main job of cleaning toxins and waste from Pembroke's body is done in Hepatic Mountain," Patty explains.

"Wow!" Arthur says in amazement.

"That's only the beginning," Patty says. "Hepatic Mountain stores energy and makes that bile we kayaked through that digests food in Pembroke's intestines. The mountain also helps Pembroke's blood to clot."

"This is a very important place for keeping Pembroke healthy," Arthur concludes.

"Very important, indeed."

He paddles onward around small boulders that have fallen in the duct from Hepatic Mountain.

"I don't remember seeing these rocks when we paddled through the first part of the common bile duct. Where did they all come from?"

"Uh-oh!" Patty says in a worried voice. "This could be trouble."

Before Arthur can ask what the trouble is, they hear the sound of more falling rocks. Patty tells Arthur to put his safety helmet on and paddle the kayak hard right so they can turn around and get out of Hepatic Mountain before it's too late. Soon they are out of the mountain, but more rocks keep piling up in the common bile duct.

"What's happening?" Arthur yells over his shoulder to Patty as he paddles as fast as he can around the boulders.

"It's not our lucky day, Arthur. These stones seem to be flowing out of the gall bladder too! Everything's clogging up. We're going to be trapped in the middle. Pembroke's poor eating habits over the years have allowed calcium stones to develop in his gall bladder. And now the stones are rolling into the common bile duct, blocking Arthur and Paddy from escaping back to the digestive system. They are indeed trapped in the bile duct, not able to advance or retreat.

"Now what are we going to do?"

"With this bile duct plugged up, there isn't much we can do, except hope and pray," Patty explains. "Soon Pembroke's bile will start backing up. When that happens, Pembroke is going to feel pain like he's never felt before."

"Pembroke can stand lots of pain! So, what's the problem?" Arthur says after mentally reviewing all of the textbook knowledge on the subject he's learned at Pepsin Academy.

"I don't think Pembroke's ever felt the pain of having an organ fail!"

"Oh-my-gosh— organ failure! We're all going to die! Buried here forever! I won't get to see—"

Before Arthur finishes his sentence, they hear Pembroke whining.

"I think that's his Hepatic Mountain beginning to shut down!" Patty observes.

All of a sudden their whole world begins bouncing around, turning upside down. Arthur and Patty toss over, right side up and upside down, until everything suddenly comes to a standstill.

"What happened?" Arthur howls at the top of his lungs.

"I think Pembroke fell down. This isn't good," Patty says as calmly as possible.

A few seconds later Arthur says, "What's that rumbling? Everything is quivering and quaking!"

"Those quivers and quakes are vibrations. I think that's good news."

"Why do you think those vibrations are good news, Patty?"

"Because they feel like the vibrations coming from the wheels of a car. I've felt those kinds of vibrations before, when I was in the intestines of human beings when they were being taken to hospitals."

"That's right! I know those vibrations, too, from when Pembroke goes on vacation with the Monroe family. What's a hospital?"

"It's a place where humans go to get medical and surgical treatment and care when they are sick or injured. I think we are going to a pet hospital where Pembroke can be surgically treated and cared for," Patty states, making it as simple as she can for Arthur.

"Surgical treatment?"

"You play Surgery, right? Well, sometimes dogs have to have something surgically removed from them by a veterinarian to make them feel better."

"Veterinarian?"

"Yeah, 'vet' for short. A vet is a pet doctor that takes care of sick and injured dogs," Patty replies.

"Doctor? What's a doctor?"

"A doctor is the title given a vet that shows he or she has been trained to care for or to perform surgery on dogs. Don't you have trained doctors at Der Kot University?"

"No. Der Kot University doesn't have programs for training doctors. If they did, I would know."

"Interesting. Arthur, have you noticed the vibrations have stopped."

"No. I hadn't notice the vibrations stopping. What do you think that means?"

"I have no idea. Let's just wait and see."

After what seems like a very long time to bacteria

and viruses, strange new vibrations are felt. Arthur can't identify what the sounds are. The sounds are very familiar to Patty, who has been in operating rooms many times before.

"Pembroke has fur and skin around his body like you have jelly and a capsule around your body. It sounds like the vet is shaving off Pembroke's fur and is cutting through his skin."

"Oh, the vet is playing the game of Surgery?" Arthur guesses.

"No. This time the vet is playing Surgery for real," Patty informs Arthur.

Again, after what seems like a long period of bacterial time, Patty and Arthur again feel violent vibrations that almost shake them out of the kayak.

"What's that!" Arthur screams out.

"That, my friend, is the sound of the vet's scalpel slicing through the passageway behind our kayak. See the bright light?" Patty observes.

"It's blinding! I've never seen a bright light like that before," Arthur says.

"The bright light comes from operating room lights that the vet uses to better see what he's doing."

"What's happening?" Arthur asks nervously.

"I don't know exactly what's happening!" Patty confesses.

Patty and Arthur see the tips of tweezers remove boulders from behind them. The way is open and cleared of stones. Neither of them know where that opening leads.

"Let's get out of here," Arthur exerts.

"Wait a second!" Patty cautions.

The tweezers clamp the opening shut, and all is dark within Pembroke's common bile duct. *Snip!* The vibration from the scissors cutting through Pembroke's bile duct is felt in front of the kayak. Blinding lights are again seen at the other end of the duct. The vet lifts the snipped duct and looks for tiny stones clogging Pembroke's bile duct.

"What is that?" Arthur screams.

"That, Arthur, is the eyeball of the vet, I imagine. Hold on tight, Arthur!" Patty warns.

The pressure of the vet's tweezers forces the kayak and Arthur and Patty out of the snipped duct into the bright lights of the operating room. The last sight they see is the vet's eyeball, as the operating room lights completely blind them. Arthur experiences for the first time in his life the feelings of a brand new environment. And he likes it.

"Hooray, we're in the Great Expanse!" shouts Arthur.

"Only for a moment!" Patty says as they tumble back into Pembroke's abdominal cavity. "Hold on to the kayak, Arthur, or we'll be lost for sure!"

Arthur takes a hold of the kayak with both hands as it falls safely into Pembroke's cavity. T cells, NK cells, and antibodies fly by, like waves of fighter jets. The few germs that get into Pembroke's body are immediately neutralized by Pembroke's immune system. Arthur and Patty escape unharmed under the shadow of Pembroke's rib cage. They watch in horror and amazement as the last of the germs are killed off by Pembroke's immune system.

"Your cloaking device works well, Patty! We're alive!" Arthur exclaims in exhilarated relief. His relief is short-lived, though, as he is almost knocked off the kayak by the vet squirting saline solution into Pembroke's body cavity before suturing the dog's surgical wound.

"What's happening to us, Patty? I've lost control of the kayak!"

"It's the flood of saline solution! Hold on, Arthur. Here we go again!"

"I can't see a thing! Paddle hard left, Arthur! Quickly!" commands Patty.

Arthur drowns his paddle deep and hard on the right side of the kayak, turning it around. But the raging water sucks them backward.

Chapter 7

BATTLE OF PIRATE'S COVE

PATTY AND Arthur's screams are lost in the turbulent flood of saline solution. But as fast as the raging waters started, once more all is calm. The kayak spins softly in the Serous Sea. Arthur paddles north with Patty securely attached on his back. They slip unnoticed in the clear, pale-yellow waters between the magnificent reddish-brown Hepatic Mountains and Pembroke's stomach. Overhead, the last of the NK cells, T cells, and Y-shaped antibodies silently pass by on the way to their bases in Pembroke's bones and thymus.

"There's the pancreas. Paddle the kayak toward the narrow tail of the organ, so we can tie up and explore," Patty commands.

"Explore what?" asks Arthur.

"The Islands of Langerhans," Patty responds.

"Oh no, here we go again! I don't know if I can take any more excitement, Patty! I get the heebie-jeebies every time we paddle to a new place," Arthur exclaims.

"Grow up, Arthur! Are you a bacterium or a chicken?"

Arthur thinks long and hard about the choices Patty gives him. He longs for the quiet and certainty of his home and school and family and friends. But at some deep level, he truly loves the excitement of exploring new lands. Patty's head slap wakes him up.

"I'm a bacterium!" Arthur declares in a loud voice.

"Okay, then get out of the kayak and tie us up to the tail of the pancreas," Patty orders.

On shore, Arthur asks, "Do I need to take a lunch?"

"No," Patty replies, "We'll be back before noon. Let's go."

Patty leads the way up the organ and finds a small crack in the neck of Pembroke's pancreas.

"This doesn't look good."

"What doesn't look good?" Arthur asks in a high-pitched, nervous voice.

"I don't know what exactly is happening. Pembroke may have injured himself. We'll find out more as we descend into him and do a more careful examination."

Arthur, with Patty on his back, ventures deeper and deeper into Pembroke's pancreas.

"It's getting warmer the deeper we go," Patty observes.

"I've never seen this kind of weather in Pembroke before," Arthur says.

"Look how red the tissue is! It's almost glowing."

"I've never seen that before either. What's happening?"

"The tissue seems to be swollen; it looks painful to touch."

"What's going on, Patty?" Arthur asks, almost beside himself.

"Pembroke is showing signs of pancreatitis."

"What's that?"

"That, my friend, is big trouble," Patty answers seriously. "Pancreatitis is an inflammation of the pancreas."

"Inflammation!"

"That's what we are seeing here. His pancreas is red and swollen, hot like we're feeling, and I'm sure at some point it will be painful to Pembroke."

"What caused Pembroke to become inflamed?" Arthur asks.

"I was just thinking about that. I don't think he's infected, because we don't see any evidence of germs. Pembroke's immune system did a great cleanup of all the germs. Hum, that means Pembroke could have injured his pancreas when he went into shock and fell down. Maybe the vet's scalpel or scissors nicked his pancreas during surgery. Possibly his pancreas simply isn't working well after all these years. Who knows?"

"It could have been the anesthesia and those tranquillizers given to Pembroke at the pet hospital. I know I was feeling a little woozy," Arthur contributes.

"That's another possibility. Trying to process the drugs given to him at the hospital could have damaged his pancreas. Now that you mention it, I did detect the Pentothal used to put Pembroke out, and something else that doesn't quite come to mind yet … That's it! There's a faint taste of Clomipramine and a bit of Rimadyl, I'd say. What do you think, Arthur?"

"I really wouldn't know, Patty. I've been stuck in Pembroke's bowels all of my life. By the time anything gets to me, it's all been broken down into waste. Why do you ask?"

"I think the medicines Pembroke's been taking may be causing the problems he had in Hepatic Mountain and may be causing his problems here.

"Great! That's just great! Let's get out of here before this place falls apart."

"Go if you need to, but I need to do what I can to remedy Pembroke's problems."

Arthur doesn't leave. He doesn't say a word and follows Patty deeper into the pancreas until they are on the surface of the main pancreatic duct.

"We'll stop here. This is a great vantage point to see the Islands of Langerhans and watch what's going on."

"We are just going to sit here and watch? Watch for what, Patty?"

"Watch for anything that catches our eyes, Arthur. You watch what's happening on the left side of the pancreatic duct, and I'll check out the right side."

"What are those things? They are all over the pancreas. They look like clusters of flowers oozing nectar."

"Those are the Islands of Langerhans, which produce powerful enzymes that flow to the common bile duct through the pancreatic duct we're sitting on."

"Oh," Arthur says taking it all in.

Patty continues, "There are hundreds and hundreds of thousands of those islands in Pembroke's pancreas, maybe millions. And they're all producing enzymes to digest food. Remember all the green stuff dripping out of the Sphincter of Oddi?"

"Oh yeah, I remember. That's the green stuff that digests fats, carbohydrates, and proteins in the chyme we saw coming out of Acid Lake. Patty! Look over there by the third branching bile duct. That dark area ..."

"That may be the source of Pembroke's problem. I believe you've found Pirate's Cove."

"What's that?" Arthur reacts.

"That's the name I give places where I've seen enzymes escaping from the Islands of Langerhans in mammals I've infected."

"Mammals? What's a mammal?"

"That's the name human scientists give to warm-blooded animals with backbones like Pembroke. I'll tell you all about them when we get back home. Trust me for now—Pembroke's in real trouble."

"What do you mean, 'real trouble'?"

"Like you said, Arthur, enzymes digest the fats, carbohydrates, and proteins in Pembroke's chyme. They are very powerful but harmless when kept inside Pembroke's pancreas, ducts, and intestines. But once enzymes get outside of those areas, they can't tell the difference between food and Pembroke's organs. They'll digest everything they touch, including Pembroke's kidneys, spleen, heart, and anything else they reach. They'll even digest Pembroke's Hepatic Mountain, if they get that far. Let's close in and see what's going on."

Patty and Arthur climb down and lay flat on the island cliff overlooking the cove. They watch the dark area below. Hundreds of enzymes are pouring out of the cove and setting off across the Pancreatic Seas to the other islands.

"If those pirating enzymes reach the other Islands of Langerhans, they will digest them and eventually digest their way out of the pancreas. Outside of the pancreas, who knows what they will do."

"That's terrible. And there goes Pembroke," Arthur says fearfully.

"The good news is I don't observe any blood in the

Pancreatic Seas, so the pirates have not digested any capillaries or blood vessels. And the front pirates are only quarter way to the next island, so we have time to act."

"Let's go down and kill 'em all, Patty!"

"Probably not a good idea, Arthur. The pirate enzymes are not technically alive and, therefore, cannot be killed in the usual way."

"How about turning up the heat in Pembroke and boiling the suckers to death?"

"Pembroke would be heated to the same boiling temperature too."

"Not a good idea," Arthur admits.

"True," Patty agrees. "If we can catch up with them, we can transform their DNA."

"Genetically transform them?" Arthur says.

"Yes, we can give them a new set of genes that will give them a new set of instructions to follow so they will act to help and not destroy the pancreas—turn them from evil to good so they can become beneficial to Pembroke."

"Oh, and just how are we going to do that and not get ourselves digested by the pirates?"

"We are going to sneak up on them, and you are going to swap your good DNA for their bad DNA. That will stop them from digesting the pancreas and stop them from killing Pembroke."

"What!" Arthur shouts excitedly. "What happens

to me when I have the pirate's bad DNA inside of me?"

"Relax, my friend. Bacteria swap DNA all the time. The bad DNA will not affect you at all."

"Why doesn't the bad DNA affect me?"

"Human scientists haven't figured that one out. However, the bad DNA does not seem to affect bacteria like you. Believe me. You know in your heart it's true, Arthur."

"What's a heart?" Arthur says, but deep inside he knows what Patty is talking about.

Arthur takes time to think things through. He knows Patty is right and asks her about the rest of the plan to attack the pirates.

"How are we going to sneak up on them?"

"You're a sociable bacterium and you're invisible."

"Oh, I forgot I was invisible," Arthur remembers.

"We'll swim alongside them, attract their attention, and make friends with them. Before they know it, you will have swapped DNA with them."

"Your idea is that I, one bacterium with a virus on my back, swim right up to a thousand cutthroat pirates and charm them?"

"No, I'm talking about thousands and thousands of you and me swimming up to a thousand or so cutthroats and you charming them and swapping DNA with them."

"How does that work?"

"You reproduce by binary fission, don't you?"

"Binary fission?" Arthur repeats with a 'huh?' look on his face.

"It means you reproduce by splitting in two. Isn't that how Honey or the professor made you?"

"Oh yeah," Arthur says, remembering how he was made.

"Which reminds me, why haven't you begun to reproduce your own kind by binary fission?"

Arthur thinks for a whole minute, figuring out an answer to Patty's question.

"I guess I'm still in my lag phase, still adjusting to my new environment," he responds.

"Well then, it's about time you stop lagging and get going. Let's start dividing and multiplying!"

Arthur divides himself in two.

"Now there are two of us, Patty."

"That's a start. Keep going! Faster, Arthur, faster!"

Arthur keeps dividing as fast as he can: four, eight, sixteen, thirty-two bacteria. In an hour and thirty-six minutes, 4096 invisible lavender Arthurs with orange-topped Pattys on their backs are on the island cliff above Pirate's Cove—far more than enough to charm, overwhelm, and swap out the bad genes from the fifteen hundred cutthroat pirates streaming out of Pirate's Cove plus those swimming to reach the closest Island of Langerhans.

"First, we have to stop that leak of enzymes coming out of the cove below us," Patty directs.

"Right-O, Patty-O," Arthur says with glee.

Patty and Arthur lead their legion of lavender-orange bacteria into Pirate's Cove.

"Hello, Mr. Pirate," Arthur says to the first enzyme he meets. "My name is Arthur Bacterium. I'm lavender and happy to meet you. And I'd like you to meet my best friend Patty. She's an orange virus that's attached to my back."

"What! Who! Where are you?"

"I'm right in front of you, Mr. Pirate," Arthur says, stifling his laughter. "Would you help me repair the leaks in your Island of Langerhans?"

The pirate enzyme looks in the direction of Arthur's voice and boasts, "I'm going to digest your sorry little lavender body, you bacteria twerp! And eat that little orange virus on your back for dessert!"

Arthur slams into the pirate enveloping the enzyme in his gelatinous covering. The enzyme looks startled, but appears to like being caught in Arthur's jelly. That's when Arthur transfers his friendly genes to the enzyme. Immediately, the cutthroat pirate enzyme changes its ferocious pirate's tune.

"Excuse me, Mr. Bacterium, and you too, Miss Patty," says the former cutthroat pirate. "I don't know what made me say that. I'm so sorry for my rude behavior. Can you ever forgive me?"

Arthur glances in Patty's direction and thinks, *What do you know about that! This swapping my genetic stuff with the enzyme works like a charm!*

"Nice to meet you," Patty says to the good pirate enzyme. "I accept your apology, sir."

"Most certainly, my good friend," adds Arthur. "We all have bad days ever so often. I forgive you too, kind sir. Best of luck to you."

While Arthur and Patty pleasantly exchange their DNA with one pirate after another, the same DNA gene swapping process is going on between Arthur and Patty's thousands and thousands of reproductions and the rest of the band of pirates on the island. In no time flat, the reformed pirates join Patty and Arthur and their legion of reproductions in sealing off Pirate's Cove. Pembroke's own healing process will take care of the finer points of rebuilding and reconnecting his pancreatic tissues.

"Thanks for all your help," Arthur calls to the ex-pirates.

"And a good day to you, sir, and Miss Patty too," the reformed pirates call back to Arthur as they bounce joyfully around in the shallows of the Pancreatic Sea. They wave good-bye and cheer Arthur and Patty and the legion on their way in pursuit of the remaining pirate enzyme swimming toward the next Island of Langerhans.

Patty, Arthur, and their legion quickly encircle the

enzyme pirates, who have no clue where their friendly voices are coming from. The result is the same as it was at Pirate's Cove. Angry, violent pirates bent on digesting everything in Pembroke turn to mellow, jolly fellows as their natures are changed from bad to good. Within minutes the victory is complete without killing a single pirate. All hostilities cease. Pembroke is saved.

Patty and Arthur return to the shores of the pancreas and look out over the Pancreatic Sea, which teems with thousands of Patty's and Arthur's reproductions and thousands of happy former pirate enzymes—all dedicated to protecting Pembroke's pancreas for years to come.

Patty smiles at Arthur. "Did you notice that our reproductions haven't been attacked by Pembroke's immune system?"

"I guess your cloaking device will genetically transfer to each new generation of our bacteria-viruses reproductions. And that's a good thing."

"Absolutely! We've created a new species of microorganism. I find that fascinating," Patty comments. "The battle was ours from the start because you are so good and charming."

Arthur blushes.

"Thank you," he replies.

Arthur follows his own footsteps, backtracking through the pancreas and out of the crack in the organ's surface. They rest on the shore of the Serous Sea and fall asleep, dreaming of their triumph at Pirate's Cove and all of their reproductions left in the Pancreatic Sea. The next morning, Arthur unties the kayak.

"What do you want to do next?" Patty asks.

"I've never been in Pembroke's circulatory system."

"That's a good idea, Arthur. Let's take the kayak back to the Pancreatic Sea and figure out how to get into the bloodstream."

Arthur carries the kayak back through the crack in the surface of the pancreas. He skillfully maneuvers down to the warm waters of the Pancreatic Sea, where he carefully places the kayak.

"That was close," Arthur says. "I saw signs of the crack in Pembroke's pancreas healing shut."

"He's a very resilient dog for being seven years old. With his healing powers, Pembroke will be around for a long, long time."

Once again, Arthur and Patty paddle through the cheering, waving crowds of their reproductions and the good pirates, and they work their way into a branch of an artery that takes them upstream. They will never forget the fifteen hundred good enzyme pirates and Arthur and Patty's lavender-orange topped creations left behind to protect Pembroke.

Paddling as fast as he can, Arthur reaches the splendid artery that leads to the abdominal aorta.

"What's that rumbling sound?"

"Our next adventure," Patty says as Arthur paddles

into Pembroke's turbulent aorta. Bright maroon–colored blood cells about the size of Arthur and a few larger white cells whiz by the kayak. Invisible and safely cloaked from view, Arthur and Patty are safe from attack, but being hit by one of these blood cells or by other bits of other stuff flying through the aorta would spoil their vacation.

"I'm losing control of the kayak!" Arthur yells.

"Okay, here we go again, Arthur!" Patty yells back through the deafening sound of the turbulence.

Chapter 8

RENAL FALLS

"THERE'S THE renal artery. Make a hard right!" Patty commands.

Arthur knows to react quickly to Patty's directions, as delay usually means disaster. The rush of aortic plasma sweeps them into the renal artery. Inside the kidney, Patty and Arthur are roughed up as they are slammed against the millions of nephrons that remove urea from the blood. The noise is thunderous.

"Grab on to the side of one of the nephrons so we won't be torn apart!"

"What was that Patty?" Arthur shouts, trying to hear Patty, who is still riding on his back.

"The pressure is tearing us apart!"

"I can't hear you," Arthur shouts back.

Patty can't hear Arthur either. Spinning left and

then right, round and round, and sometimes rolling over and over, they can do nothing to stop being drawn closer to Renal Falls and the mighty Urine River that flows out of Pembroke!

"We're trapped in a one-way collecting tube, heading for the falls. Try digging into the sides of the tube," Patty screams as loud as she can from Arthur's back.

He focuses on the vibrations coming from Patty's lips. Putting the vibrations together, he is able to get the idea of what she wants him to do. Arthur tries clawing into the collecting tube. Then, miracle of miracles, he manages to dig into the tube, clinging on for his life.

"I've done it, Patty, I've done it!"

But Patty can't hear him, because she has been torn from Arthur's back. Patty and the kayak are tumbling toward the falls, leaving Arthur hanging all alone. Renal Falls come up fast for Patty, as she braces herself in the kayak before going over.

"I'm not afraid. I'm not afraid. I'm not afraid," Patty keeps saying to herself.

Arthur clings on to the collecting tube as long as he can. Soon he loses his grip and drops headlong through the convoluted tube to the top of the falls.

"Patty! Patty!" Arthur cries in vain, but no response is heard.

Fortunately, Patty and the kayak have already splashed down safely in Bladder Lake. Swimming to the kayak, she climbs in and patiently waits for Arthur to drop in.

"Patty! Patty! Patty!" Arthur screams as he flounders at the edge of the falls. He looks over and can't see the bottom. Small stones roll by him and plunge into the abyss. Arthur takes one last look for Patty. Not seeing her anywhere, he makes a decision.

I guess I'm next to go, he thinks before rolling over the falls.

Patty can hear him screaming millimeters away. *PLOOP!* A second later, with arms flailing in the air in every direction, Arthur plunges into Bladder Lake.

Surfacing, Arthur says, "Patty, Patty, I thought I'd never see you again!"

Patty smiles and helps him into the kayak. She reattaches herself to Arthur by snuggling on his back, which restarts their invisible protective shield. Paddling the lake for a few minutes, they notice the urine level creep higher and higher.

"What's happening?" Arthur asks.

"I think Bladder Lake is getting full."

"What's going to happen to us, Patty?"

"We have two choices, Arthur. We can try to hold on to the lakeshore when the lake is dumped into the Great Expanse. Or, we can stay in the kayak and take a quick trip into the Great Expanse."

"What do you mean, Patty? Except for a moment

during Pembroke's surgery, I've never been in the Great Expanse."

Before Patty can answer Arthur's question, the muscles surrounding the lake receive neurological instructions to empty Bladder Lake.

"Here we go!" Patty calls out.

"Oh no!" Arthur cries.

WHIZ! BANG! Arthur, Patty, and the kayak hit the Great Expanse.

"Hold on tight to the kayak, Arthur!" Patty shouts out.

In all of the excitement, Arthur stands up and is thrown out of the kayak. His lavender rod-shaped body lands somewhere in the grasses of the Monroe's backyard. Orange Patty flings off Arthur's back and lands somewhere else in the grass, while the kayak is flung in a different direction. They all land safely. Patty and Arthur have only vague ideas where the other has landed or where their kayak wound up.

"Arthur," Patty yells, "get out of the sun, or you will dry up and die!"

Hearing Patty, Arthur clambers under a blade of grass with lots of dewdrops hanging on its underside. He instinctively knows moving will sap his strength. He stays still, shaded in the moisture of the grass.

"Arthur," Patty cries out, "tell me if you think I'm getting closer to you."

Patty starts singing and walking in the direction where she thinks Arthur landed.

Every once in a while, Arthur calls, "You're getting closer."

"Am I closer now?" asks Patty.

"Yes, I can see you," Arthur says.

Patty looks under the blade of grass that Arthur has been using as shelter.

"There you are, Arthur."

"Here I am. What are we going to do?"

Orange Patty grabs Arthur and merges with him again to ensure her cloaking device protects him.

"Ouch, that hurt!" Arthur cries. "I think I'm drying out fast out here in the Great Expanse!"

"Stop being such a baby. I have a plan, one that will help us easily get back inside of Pembroke."

"What's the plan?"

"You see all the water vaporizing in the Great Expanse?"

"You mean the stuff rising in the air?"

"Yes. When Pembroke comes toward us, which I'm sure he will in time, he will be sniffing the ground. That's when we will ride the water vapor right up through his nose, and we'll be back home free!"

"That sounds pretty risky to me."

"So is staying here and drying out in the noonday sun! Besides, bacteria ride in and out of Pembroke every time he breathes in and out."

"Oh, now I get it! I've heard stories about this in school. Bacteria that have gone out in the Great Expanse often get back into Pembroke by riding air molecules."

"Pembroke eating dog poop is the other major way this works," elaborates Patty.

"I've never heard about bacteria getting back that way!"

"Your dad never told you dogs eat their poop?"

"No," Arthur answers quizzically.

"Oh boy! Are we in luck? I see the kayak under that mushroom."

"Mushroom? What's a mushroom?"

"Here comes Pembroke. We don't have time to play twenty questions, Arthur. Move straight ahead and fast!"

"I don't want to dry out in the sun!"

"Get going Arthur! That's a command!" Thanks to Patty steering Arthur in the right direction, he moves to the side of the kayak.

"Quick, into the kayak, Arthur."

Arthur flops over the side of the kayak just in time. Pembroke roams back through the lawn, sniffing the ground as he goes. His nosing through the grass disturbs a grasshopper, which seems to be of unbelievable size from Arthur's and Patty's perspectives.

"What is that, Patty?" Before Patty can answer, the grasshopper rubs its wings together, producing the most disturbing vibrations, which almost shake apart Patty's and Arthur's bodies and the kayak—*Erkie-Erkie-Erkie, Erkie-Erkie-Erkie, Erkie-Erkie-Erkie!*"

"What's that? Shiver my ribosomes!" a scared Arthur shouts.

"Don't worry, Arthur. We're too small for the grasshopper to find or hurt us. Stay low in the kayak and be ready for Pembroke's sniff!"

Sure enough, Pembroke pokes his nose under the mushroom and sniffs. Arthur, Patty, and the kayak are drawn up through Pembroke's nose and land in his mouth on the back of his large tongue.

"Portsmouth!" Patty declares. "It's good to be back in Pembroke."

"I never thought we'd make it; but here we are."

"Stay sharp, Arthur," Patty commands.

Arthur and Patty let the kayak slide through the saliva over the back of Pembroke's tongue down his esophagus.

"All those wavy things seem to be pushing us along," Arthur observes.

"Those wavy things are cilia. They're designed to sweep food down the esophagus to the stomach. All the saliva and mucus are simply helping everything along," Patty explains. "Don't get too comfortable. We're getting off at Thyroid Station and taking an artery up to the brain."

"You're kidding!"

"No, I'm serious. You haven't lived until you've seen the inside of Pembroke's brain."

Chapter 9

BATTLE OF TURKISH SADDLE

THYROID STATION is a short paddle from Portsmouth. Arthur carries the kayak across the station platform and squeezes into the upper thyroid artery. With Patty cheering him on, he paddles hard against the current until they reach the common carotid artery.

"Whoa! This is a fast moving stream. I don't even have to steer the kayak. Look, ma, no hands!" Arthur says.

"Keep both hands on your paddle, Arthur, and steer down the middle of the carotid. Stay alert. This artery is about to divide, and we need to take the internal carotid artery to get to the brain."

"I'm as quick as a mosquito on a hot frying pan."

"Look! On your right, mosquito boy—that's the

internal carotid artery. Quick! Lean that paddle to the left."

Arthur dips his paddle deeply on the left side of the kayak and holds it steady with both hands. The kayak narrowly makes its way into the internal carotid.

"*Wee-oh!* That was close. We sure lucked out there!" Arthur exclaims. "The current was almost too fast for me to make the turn, Patty. Sorry. Where are we? I haven't got a clue."

"Arthur, sometimes I think you'd get lost in a paper bag. We're under Pembroke's brain."

Patty and Arthur travel through an astounding number of curves that lead above the sphenoid bone, which looks like a large eagle flying under them. The convoluted folds of the brain above them appear like gray clouds gathering for a storm.

"What an awesome sight," Patty says as they course farther under Pembroke's brain.

"It seems like we've been paddling around in circles for hours," Arthur groans.

"We have. We're in the Circle of Willis, which supplies the brain with all the oxygenated blood it needs."

"And nourishment too?"

"Yes, Arthur, and nourishment too. Keep looking for a smaller artery so we can slip into Pembroke's brain. This time, try to keep your mosquito-like reflexes ready and move quicker."

Arthur paddles along until Patty says, "Up there, ahead. That's a good place. Take the next small artery to the left."

This time Arthur is on top of the situation and expertly guides the kayak into the tiny hole.

"Excellent, mosquito boy. Things are going to get a little rough when we hit the brain's barrier."

"Barrier?"

"Yes, the ménages. The ménages is the barrier that surrounds the whole brain and spinal cord and protects them from getting injured from being knocked around too much."

"And from being infected by bacteria and viruses like us," Arthur comments.

"Exactly. The three layers of the ménages may be a big challenge for our cloaking device. Pembroke's brain is a large computer that controls everything in Pembroke. It's protected by the highest security—very, very tough. Like nothing we've ever seen before."

Arthur feels a pain in his gut. If the cloaking device fails, he will never see South Pembroke or his family and friends again.

"I'm paddling to pick up speed so we can crash through the tough part of the ménages," Arthur shouts.

Patty advises Arthur to position the kayak at an angle so it slides between the cells in the first hard outer part of the ménages. Her strategy works, as they slide unharmed through the outer layer.

"All right! We made it through the tough part without a scratch. What are we into now? What a mess! Is this stringy stuff the brain?"

"Not quite yet, Arthur. The stringy stuff is the beginning of the second layer of the ménages. It's designed to entangle us so Pembroke's immune agents can easily pick us off."

The kayak moves up and down, left and right through what looks like a spider's web. Tangled in the webbing, Arthur and Patty see dead bacteria and viruses, chemical molecules, toxins, and old broken blood and tissue cells.

"Look at all the stuff that didn't get through to the brain. I hope we don't wind up the same way," sighs Arthur.

"Just keep paddling, Arthur, and we'll be fine. One more protective layer of the ménages to go and we'll be in the brain."

"What's this soft, spongy stuff, Patty?"

"That's the third and last layer of the ménages, called the tender mother. The spongy stuff covers the brain way down into its folds and cushions it from being knocked around against the inside of Pembroke's skull."

"What's next?"

"The Axon Sea," Patty replies.

So as to not tear the last layer of the ménages, Arthur carefully works the kayak through the tender mother. Once past the last protective layer, they find themselves submerged in a thick, straw-colored liquid.

"It feels like we're floating in space!"

"We are floating, Arthur. We're floating in the Axon Sea. Pembroke's brain and spinal cord are entirely submerged in this fluid to protect them from being shocked or damaged."

"This is fun!" Arthur squeals.

"Stay alert, mosquito boy. We're going to take a brain tour. Keep sharp! There are lots of twists and turns, dead-ends, and secret parts to Pembroke's brain. We can easily get lost in this maze."

Arthur keeps his senses wide open. If he ever wants to see his family and friends again, his intuitions tell him to listen to Patty. Witnessing all the wonders of Pembroke's brain, he paddles through the Axon Sea. Sparks appear to be flying across Pembroke's brain, lighting up some of his brain cells.

"What are all those flashing lights, Patty? I've never seen anything like that."

"It looks like lightening flashing in one of Pembroke's brainstorms."

"Lightening? Brainstorms? I don't get it."

"Those flashes traveling inside Pembroke's brain are chemical-electrical messages from all over Pembroke's body to all parts of his brain and Pembroke's brain sending chemical-electrical messages to all of Pembroke's body."

"Oh, that's how the brain controls everything Pembroke does," reasons Arthur.

"That's right. You know, bacteria don't have brains like Pembroke because bacteria don't have nervous systems."

"I know that!" Arthur says, somewhat hurt by Patty's comment. "Bacteria do have biological computers kind-of that work like a brain for the whole floral colony. A billion bacteria computers working together are just as good as a dog's brain!"

"I guess you're right. Different life-forms have their own way of controlling what they do. After all, bacteria and viruses have been around a lot longer than dogs and have done quite well."

Arthur feels a lot better after hearing Patty agree that bacteria are very important and are just as good as dogs.

"Down there, Patty. What's that?"

"That's the old puppy brain. It develops before a puppy is even born. The old brain has everything to do with Pembroke's digestion, heartbeat, swallowing, breathing, and sneezing. The old brain is totally automatic. Pembroke doesn't have to think about doing any of those activities."

"Interesting," Arthur responds. "That's how we bacterial work—on a totally automatic level. What's that over there, in front of the old puppy brain?"

"That's a newer part of the old puppy brain. It's

called the second puppy brain. Pembroke doesn't have to think about what this part of the brain does either. Pembroke's second puppy brain controls his balance, blood circulation, muscle tone, sleep, and his instincts to play fetch."

"Dogs love to play fetch. Is that why the second puppy brain is the largest part of Pembroke's brain?"

"Good guess, Arthur. Actually Pembroke's second puppy brain is larger than the old brain because it plays fetch and maintains blood circulation and muscle tone. It's bigger because it does more jobs than the old puppy brain."

"We are coming to the front of Pembroke's brain," Arthur announces.

"That large front part of Pembroke's brain is what he uses to think. Nothing is automatic there. Pembroke has to think and make sense out of what he sees, hears, feels, smells, and tastes. He has to remember what is good for him and what isn't."

"I learned in school that a dog's ears, nose, and eyes are very good—better than humans, I bet!" Arthur adds.

"Yes, plus this is the part of the brain that determines Pembroke's intelligence and personality," Patty continues.

"Down there—that dark area. What's going on there?" Arthur asks.

"That's the area called the Turkish Saddle, where

the pituitary gland sits protected in the bony saddle. It's hard to see what's happening. Paddle a little closer, Arthur."

For a short while, Arthur paddles toward the pituitary. Then he slows down until he comes to a stop. Motionless, Arthur and Patty peer into the darkness of Turkish Saddle.

"Doesn't the front part of the pituitary gland look larger than the rest of the gland, like something is growing on it?"

Arthur and Patty strain their eyes to clearly see as much as they can.

"Patty, I think you're right. The front part of the pituitary does look bigger."

Arthur paddles closer.

"The pituitary looks like it's moving. I think Pembroke's pituitary cells are growing—growing out of control," Patty says.

"You mean Pembroke has pituitary cancer!" Arthur responds. "I've seen pictures of cancers like that in my school books. They are very nasty."

"The cancer hasn't spread outside of the Turkish Saddle to other parts of the brain," Patty observes. "We have to stop it before it spreads."

"We'll divide ourselves and conquer the cancer cells like we did with the enzymes at Pirate's Cove!" responds Arthur.

"No, this cancer is made up of viruses, not enzymes.

I'll have to take the lead on this one," Patty asserts. "But I still need your help. It's going to be a little complicated to understand, Arthur, so listen carefully."

Arthur listens to Patty as he has never listened to anyone before, not even his parents.

"The idea is you're going to bamboozle the cancer cells while I attack them and infect them with a special protein that will kill them." Patty continues, "First, I have to take some of your waste protein and make a poison to inject into the cancer cells. Second, I have to use you to reproduce a couple million viruses."

"Like we did at Pirate's Cove?" Arthur replies.

"Yes, but this time I need to infect you so you can reproduce about two million orange poison viruses that look like me."

"Will I die in the process?"

"No, you won't die. But I do need you to lead fifty thousand of the poison viruses into battle against the cancer cells."

"We'll be outnumbered twenty to one," Arthur whines.

"True, but the cancer cells will never reach you. Listen closely."

"Okay," Arthur says, trying to compose himself.

"I need you to attack the cancer cells head-on until you hear me sound the retreat. It will feel like the vibrations the large grasshopper made when we were in the Great Expanse."

"I remember that huge insect flying over us when Pembroke was sniffing through the grass," Arthur says.

"Exactly." Patty continues, "When you hear the retreat sound, you and your fifty thousand viruses turn and run. That's when I and the rest of the poison viruses will rush in and destroy the cancer cells."

Arthur listens and understands the plan, but he doesn't like it.

"Let me see if I got this right," Arthur exclaims. "First, you're going inside me to get protein to make into a poison to use to infect and kill a million cancer cells?"

"I don't have to go inside of you to get the protein material. I'll use the protein material you've already excreted. Your poo makes a beautiful poison that I will use to modify the cancer's genetic materials and change them," Patty explains.

"Where are you going to get that much of my poo to make all the poison you'll need to arm two million orange viruses?" Arthur asks.

"You've left a lot of excrement in the kayak. I'll use that."

"Okay, that takes a lot off my mind—good. But then you are going to use me to reproduce over two million viruses. That sounds like it's going to hurt?"

"It's not going to hurt, Arthur. We've created reproductions before in the pancreas, and you were fine," Patty assures Arthur.

"Okay, I'll buy that. Why am I leading only fifty thousand viruses into battle against millions of cancer cells," Arthur says uneasily. "How's that supposed to work?" Arthur asks on the edge of hysteria. "I'm beginning to panic a little!"

"Settle down. Breathe deeply through your cell wall and let the air slowly go out of you. Calm down. Everything will be fine. You won't be hurt or killed in the process. I guarantee you that much."

Arthur breathes deeply several times as Patty comforts him. He lets the air out slowly. He feels much better as Patty's words soothe him.

Patty continues, "Arthur, when you take fifty thousand killer viruses and charge the pituitary cancer cells in Turkish Saddle head-on, I and the rest of the two million orange poison viruses will be in hiding and will attack the cancer cells you lead into our trap."

"I don't know," Arthur says. "It sounds like my fifty thousand poison viruses and I die in a stupid charge against a million cancer cells. Doesn't sound like a good plan to me!" Arthur screams.

"No, Arthur, you won't die. I'll have the cancer cells flanked with a million orange viruses on each side. When they are almost on top of you, two million orange viruses will swoop down in full force and destroy the million cancer cells."

"It sounds like you're putting me and fifty thousand

viruses on a hook and dangling us like fish bait!" Arthur says, still not at all convinced Patty's plan would work.

"You are the bait to draw the cancer cells out of Turkish Saddle into the open, but I and the two million other viruses will destroy them before they reach you. It's the old pincher movement that's worked for over trillions and trillions of bacteria years."

"I don't like it. Why don't you be the bait, and I attack the flanks," Arthur insists.

"If they see me, Arthur, they won't attack. But when you show them your friendly, innocent, born-yesterday bacterium face, the cancer cells won't see you as a threat," Patty argues.

"Oh, you want the cancer cells to see me as easy pickings and attack me and my merry band of wet-behind-the-ears viruses full force! Then, when they are about to gobble up me and my gullible little friends, you spring the trap and surprise them as you sweep in for the kill!"

"You've got it, Arthur."

"I don't like it, Patty. It's too risky."

"The plan will work, Arthur. The longer we sit here and argue, the more the cancer cells will multiply!"

"And if you're late? What happens then, Patty?" Arthur says with fear showing in his eyes.

"Trust me, Arthur; I will not let you die."

"I do trust you, but I'm afraid," Arthur says.

"Oh, I forgot one thing, Arthur."

"Now what?"

"When you hear this sound—*erkie-erkie-erkie*—retreat."

"You want me and my heroic fifty thousand viruses to charge millions of cancer cells and then chicken out when we hear *erkie-erkie-erkie*?"

"You're not chickening out, Arthur. When you hear the sound of the grasshopper, you do a tactical retreat."

"Sounds like you want us to turn tail and run like scared rabbits!"

"Okay, Arthur, have it your way." Patty exaggerates to make her point, "Charge, don't turn and run, die, and then I'll attack. Now that I think of it, that will work better. The cancers will be distracted by you and your merry band being slaughtered!"

At first, Arthur doesn't understand that Patty is joking. He's too busy ranting about being chicken and running like a rabbit and being killed.

"Oh, that's just peachy keen. Do you want us to drop our weapons, fall on our backs, whimper like dogs, and beg for mercy?" Arthur snaps back.

Patty doesn't respond to Arthur's hysteria. She waits silently for him to calm down. Finally, Arthur understands what Patty has been trying to explain to him. He realizes he'd rather be a live tactician than a dead duck.

"Okay, I get it, Patty, I understand. At the *erkie-*

erkie-erkie sound, we are going to turn our bumpkin faces and run like the wind, while you will swoop in for the kill."

"That's right, Arthur. Oh, one more thing …"

"Now what!"

"If our plan works well, we will all break off the attack and let Pembroke's immune system take over and finish the kill."

"Why? The battle is ours!"

"It's better for Pembroke's immune system to win the Battle of Turkish Saddle, so he can build up his immune strength. We can't stay here to protect him the rest of his life. Pembroke has to do that for himself."

"Sorry. I was being selfish. You're right, Patty. We need to keep our egos out of this and think of keeping Pembroke's virus and bacterium count at a safe level," Arthur says shamefully.

Patty infects Arthur with his own waste material to produce the poison protein that will kill the cancer cells. She begins the reproducing process. Seven hours later, Patty's reproduced 2,097,153 orange viruses armed with poison—more than enough to overwhelm and destroy the million-plus cancer cells, growing in Turkish Saddle.

"Are you ready to lead the charge?" Patty calls to Arthur.

He nods his head. Patty signals the attack. Arthur and his fifty thousand orange viruses turn and face

Turkish Saddle where the pituitary cancer cells lay in wait.

"Charge!" Arthur shouts at the top of his lungs as he leads his troops into battle.

The once million cancer cells have grown in numbers to a million and a half cancer cells. They see a measly bacterium and fifty thousand soldiers charging them. The cancer leaders laugh at such a weak, stupid attack. Full force, they countercharge the small band. Arthur and his fifty thousand see the storm of cancer cells descending upon them.

Arthur thinks, *They took the bait! Where's that grasshopper call!*

There is no call, as Patty is waiting until the last moment before sounding the retreat. The cancer cells descend faster on the small band of warriors. Arthur and the fifty thousand continue the charge. Just when it seems Arthur's band is sure to be slaughtered, they hear the retreat sounded.

"Erkie-Erkie-Erkie, Erkie-Erkie-Erkie, Erkie-Erkie-Erkie!"

Arthur and his fifty thousand troops come to a screeching halt. They wheel around and run for their lives in the opposite direction.

Thinking they have the enemy on the run, the million and a half cancer cells relentlessly pursue Arthur and his tiny band of viruses. The cancer cells don't notice Patty's orange poison forces swarm their flanks until it is too late. Catching the cancer cells by complete surprise, seven hundred fifty thousand cancer cells are killed in the first strike, leaving the other seven hundred fifty thousand cancer cells dazed and confused on the battlefield. Patty and her orange poison viruses swoop in and engage the remaining cancer cells in hand-to-hand combat. When the cancer cells are almost annihilated, Patty calls off the attack. Waves of Pembroke's antibodies and killer cells continue the attack.

Patty and Arthur retreat to the top of a gray convolution on Pembroke's forebrain and watch Pembroke's immune system mop-up the enemy cancer cells.

"Arthur?"

"Yes, Patty."

"How do you feel now that the battle is over?"

"Pretty good, Patty. Why shouldn't I feel good after winning a victory that saved Pembroke and my family?"

"I was just wondering if you thought the battle was worth risking your life the way you did."

"For the sake of Pembroke and my family, what does sacrificing one life matter."

"You willingly went into battle without my invisible protective shield?"

"I know," confesses Arthur. "I took a big risk, but the plan wouldn't have worked without my friendly, innocent, born-yesterday bacterium face leading the charge."

"You're such a brave bacterium, Arthur. I know your parents would be proud of you."

Patty climbs on Arthur's back and reattaches herself to activate the invisible protective shield. Later, they slip away in their kayak. Arthur and Patty's kayak gently flows into Maroon Lake, which takes them southward. They rest, floating slowly through Pembroke's Maroon River. As they hear the valves close behind them, they dream about the wonders of Pembroke's brain and their great victory at the Battle of Turkish Saddle.

"What's that roaring sound I hear?" Arthur asks.

"Nothing to be concerned about, Arthur. We're just approaching Pembroke's heart."

"Oh no!"

"Get ahold of yourself, germ! And stay alert!"

Chapter 10

BRIGHTER MAROON RIVER

ARTHUR PADDLES down the middle of the Maroon River into Pembroke's right atrium.

"Where are we?"

"We're in one of Pembroke's heart chambers and about to go through his lungs to pick up some oxygen, Arthur. Get ready for a rough ride through the Corazón River. You ain't seen nothin' yet!"

"Ouch!" Arthur yells as the force of the blood filling up the atrium creates pressure on his eardrums. "My ears are about to burst!"

Swoosh! The right atrium contracts and shoots Arthur, Patty, and the kayak into the right ventricle.

"Help me, mommy!" Arthur blurts out.

Whoosh! The right ventricle contracts, jetting

Arthur, Patty, and the kayak through the pulmonary artery into the lungs.

"I'm upside down!" Arthur shouts.

Pembroke's expanding lungs bring oxygen to the blood, turning the Corazón River a brighter shade of maroon.

"Pretty," Patty remarks as the kayak bounces around like a rubber ball.

"Ay, caramba!" Arthur screams.

They splash down and dribble through the slow-moving blood in the pulmonary artery to the left atrium, which gives Arthur and Patty time to straighten out before entering the left ventricle.

"Did you like the roller-coaster ride through the lungs?" Patty asks.

"I feel sick to my stomach," Arthur replies. "I think I'm going to throw up."

"Wait, Arthur, there's more to come."

Before Arthur has a chance to say anything, they are propelled with the force of a rocket out of the left ventricle, leaving the Corazón River behind. The strong force of the Brighter Maroon River almost drowns them as Arthur tries to control the kayak. Soon Arthur regains composure, allowing him to steadily steer down the middle of the Brighter Maroon River.

"How did you like your trip through Corazón River country, Arthur?"

Concentrating on keeping the kayak straight in

the river, Arthur answers, "Once is enough for me. Exciting, but I prefer the good old quiet of Southern Pembroke."

Patty laughs and says, "Right, Arthur! We're homeward bound now."

"That's it? My summer's over?"

"Almost—but not quite yet. We still have a ways to go."

"I can hardly wait to tell everybody about my daring ventures outside the digestive system. None of my friends have been beyond the transverse colon, let alone the Great Expanse."

"Heads up! We're in the deep, fast moving currents of the Brighter Maroon River, so stay sharp!"

They pass like a shot through Pembroke's thorax.

"Patty, look at all those turns off the river. Shouldn't we be taking one of those to get home?"

"No, Arthur. Those arteries lead to the esophagus and ribs. We'd never get home that way. Hold steady."

Speeding through the abdominal cavity, the Brighter Maroon River is strong and its currents dangerous.

"Arthur," Patty warns, "if we go too far, we will miss our station and be swept past South Port into Pembroke's legs and wind up in one of the Paw Cities. Keep an eye open for the artery to First Street."

"Is it that one, Patty?"

"No, that artery goes to the right kidney."

"Is this the one, Patty?"

Arthur anxiously paddles by several arteries, but they all lead to the small intestines.

"There! That one on the right—take it, Arthur!" Patty exclaims.

Arthur expertly guides the kayak down the medial sacral artery.

"Stop at the First Street Caudal Station."

Arthur dutifully stops at the station.

"Wow, Patty! First Street is a short walk from Canal Street, to Grove Street, and then home. Hooray! Hooray! We made it!" Arthur cries so excitedly he almost falls out of the kayak.

Patty disconnects from Arthur's back and grabs the bow rope of the kayak and ties it to the dock cleat. She helps Arthur climb safely from the kayak onto the dock.

"You won't be needing my protection anymore," Patty says.

"That's right. I'm back home again and feel like a new bacterium, Patty."

"You didn't like being under my protection, Arthur?"

"Oh no, I loved being under your protection. But a bacterium has to be a bacterium."

"Yes, I know, Arthur."

Lifting the kayak out of the river, they carry it overhead along First and Canal Streets.

"I can't wait to get home, Patty. The Great Brown River looks so fresh and inviting."

"We don't have time for a swim today, Arthur."

"I know—but I can wish, can't I?"

Patty smiles as they turn up Grove Street to the front door of Arthur's home. Placing the kayak on the front lawn, Arthur and Patty hug, ring the doorbell, and excitedly wait for the door to open. Honey answers the door with tears in her eyes. She hugs Patty and Arthur. The professor, who is just returning from the university, runs up the pathway to his home and embraces the whole family in his big arms.

"Glad to have you home, son," Arthur's dad says, picking up his wonderful lavender rod of a son. He picks up tiny orange Patty with another arm. "Great to have you back home, Patty," the professor says, patting Arthur and Patty on their backs with four of his other arms.

"Oh, the stories you two must have to tell," Honey says before running back to put dinner on the table.

"Yes, Mom, and none of this would have happened if Patty wouldn't have been there to guide me. She really knows her way around Pembroke."

They sit at the dinner table, say grace, and begin to eat while a contented Patty watches.

"Well, son," the professor begins, "tell us about your big adventure in Pembroke."

Arthur describes every thrill and every harrowing

event from the time they waved good-bye at the school grounds to the time he rang the doorbell. Patty smiles and glories in the thought that she made it possible for Arthur to experience the greatest adventure of his lifetime. She enjoys the excitement in his eyes as he tells his story to Honey and the professor.

Every night before going to bed, the family shares stories. Honey tells about growing up in Pembroke's appendix. Patty amazes the family with memories of her childhood, growing up a Nelson Virus. The professor keeps the rest of his family and Patty enthralled with his most recent discoveries about Pembroke. And, as you might expect, Arthur spins yarns about the greatest adventure of his life. To be sure, he always tells the story about his venture in the Great Expanse. As the professor listens carefully to his son's stories, he takes notes and makes a map showing the places where his son and Patty traveled. When Honey and the professor invite Patty to continue staying with them as a member of their family and live in their guest room, Patty jumps at the offer.

Arthur and Patty's last year at Pepsin Academy goes by in a flash. They attend Der Kot University—a forty-eight hour program that they finish in twenty-four hours! Patty is continually offered opportunities to be placed in higher grades and take more advanced classes, but she always turns them down. She prefers to be with Arthur. After graduation, Der Kot University insists that Arthur and Patty lead a scientific expedition into the Great Expanse. They accept in a heartbeat.

So the professor's wish that his son would explore the Great Expanse with Patty came true. Honey and the professor, Arthur's proud parents, couldn't be happier. As for Patty and Arthur, the future holds many exciting hours of adventure and exploration.

KEY TO THE PROFESSOR'S MAP

1.	Pepsin Academy	32.	Islands of Langerhans
2.	Der Kot University	33.	Kidney
3.	The Great Brown River	34.	Nephrons
4.	South Port	35.	Renal Falls
5.	Cameron Salt Plant	36.	Bladder Lake
6.	The Grove or Lunch Area	37.	Esophagus
7.	Portsmouth	38.	Cilia
8.	Lungs	39.	Thyroid Station
9.	Brighter Maroon River Express	40.	Carotid Artery
10.	Rectum Hall	41.	Internal Carotid Artery
11.	Canal Street	42.	Ascending Colon
12.	1727 Grove Street	43.	Convoluted Folds of the Brain
13.	Houston Park	44.	Circle of Willis
14.	Transverse Colon	45.	Meninges (has three parts or layers)
15.	Sigmoid Bend	46.	Tough Mother of the Meninges
16.	Hepatic Mountain Bend	47.	Spider Mother of the Meninges
17.	Cecum Hollow (remain of an appendix)	48.	Tender Mother of the Meninges
18.	Small Intestines	49.	Spinal Cord

19. Stomach	50. Axon Sea
20. Liver	51. Old Puppy Brain
21. Pancreas	52. Second Puppy Brain
22. Gall Bladder	53. Large Front Part (Frontal Lobe)
23. Descending Colon	54. Turkish Saddle/Sphenoid Bone
24. Twelve Fingers	55. Pituitary Gland
25. Sphincter of Oddi	56. Maroon Lake
26. Duodenal Curve	57. Right Atrium
27. Hepatic Mountain	58. Corazón River (flows only in the heart)
28. Common Bile Duct	59. Thorax
29. Serous Seas	60. Paw Cities (in each of Pembroke's paws)
30. Pancreatic Sea	61. Medial Sacral Artery
31. Pirate's Cove	62. First Street Caudal Station

NOTE: *The whole area around Pembroke's bottom is known as the "South or Southern Pembroke" and the whole area outside of Pembroke is known as "The Great Expanse."*

* *Dr. Louie Bacterium's diagram of the adventures of Arthur and Patty are approximations that he is drawing the diagram from the stories Arthur and Patty tell him.*

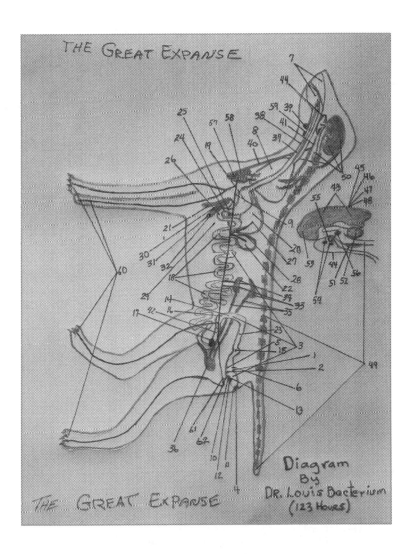

THE GREAT EXPANSE

Diagram
By
Dr. Louis Bacterium
(123 Hours)

GLOSSARY AND GUIDE
FOR PARENTS AND TEACHERS
AND CURIOUS STUDENTS

Word definitions, pronunciations, and information about key terms from the story are presented here in alphabetical order. Note: Definitions and the pronunciation of words are in part based on Microsoft Word for Mac version 11.6.0 dictionary and thesaurus; Wikipedia, the free online encyclopedia; and on *Webster's New World Dictionary*, Third College Edition, Prentice Hall (1994).

Pronunciation tips: When sounding out words in this glossary, the SHORT VOWEL SOUNDS are (a) as in *cap, fat, hat,* and *Dan*; (e) as in *get, Edgar, Mexican,* and *beck*; (i) as in *grim, thin, slim,* and *blimp*; (o) as in *rot, cop, rod,* and *rob*; and (u) as in *bug, umbrella, dug,* and *duck*. The LONG VOWEL SOUNDS are (ā) as in *ape, snail, ache, explain,* and *reindeer*; (ē) as in *eat, agony, needle, pianist,* and *electricity*; (ī) as in *eye, cry, tightrope, tile,* and *violin*; (ō) as in *oh, domino, ghost, pillow,* and *stethoscope*; and (ū) as in *you, salute, toothbrush, goose, boot,* and *costume.*

Notice: **bold print** indicates the syllable that is stressed the loudest in the word, as in "Aorta (***aa**-or-ta*)" or "Corazón River (*kor-a-**zōn** **ri**-ver*" or "Stella Turcica (***stel**-la **tur**-sē-ka*)."

abdominal aorta (*ab-**do**-me-nal ā-or-ta*): The descending aorta is called the abdominal aorta and has branches off to the kidneys, pancreas, gallbladder, liver, intestines, colon, and other tissues in the abdomen.

abdominal cavity (*ab-**do**-me-nal **kav**-i-tē*): A space within the torso, covered with the peritoneum, having the breathing muscle (diaphragm) as its top boundary, the abdominal muscles as its front boundary, lateral abdominal muscles as its side boundaries, the deep back muscles and spine as its back boundary, and the pelvic muscles at the floor of the pelvis as its bottom boundary.

absorbed (***ab**-zorbd*): Everything taken in, soaked up by the colon, the intestines, etc.

Ace: Arthur's best friend; short for *Lactobacillus acetotolerans* (*lak-tō-bak-**sil**-lus ase-tō-**tol**-er-ans*); a good stomach bacterium.

airborne (**air**-*born*): Rides the air; an airborne virus is transported by air.

Acid Lake: Another name for the acid contained in the stomach.

adventure (**ad**-*ven-chur*): An unusual, exciting, often dangerous experience or activity.

agents (**ā**-*jents*): Something or someone that works in behalf of something or someone else; in this story, agents of Pembroke's immune system are the NK (natural killer) cells, the white blood cells, and the antibodies that protect Pembroke from infection and disease; also known as Pembroke's organ police and reserves.

Al: Arthur's friend; short for *Lactobacillus alimentarius (lak-tō-bak-**sil**-lus al-lē-men-**tar**-ē-us)*.

Amy: Arthur's friend; short for *Lactobacillus amylolyticus (lak-tō-bak-**sil**-lus ā-mē-lo-**ltī**-kus)*, which can be found in beer malt and beer wort.

ancestors (**an**-*ses-tors*): Family members who predate one's grandparents.

antibodies (**an**-*ti-bod-ēs*): Protein created by in the

bloodstream that attacks toxins or foreign substances in the body.

anus (*ā-nus*): One opening to the Great Expanse; a ring muscle at the end of the anal canal of the rectum that holds food waste until one gets the urge to get rid of the food waste contained in the rectum.

anxiety (*anx-zī-e-tē*): Feeling worried, uneasy, or nervous about a coming event or something with an uncertain outcome.

aorta (*ā-or-ta*): The largest artery in the body; a major blood vessel that carries oxygenated blood (which has a brighter maroon color).

appendix (*ap-pen-diks*): A 4-inch tube attached to the *cecum* (*sē-kum*); probably a remnant of some organ used by a very remote ancestor; may store and protect good bacteria for digestion.

appetite (*ap-pe-tīt*): A signal from the body that it needs to be fed.

applause (*ap-plauz*): To show approval, happiness, or pleasure by clapping one's hands together.

Arthur Bacterium (*ar-thur bak-teer-ē-a*): One of the

two main characters in the story: the friendly lavender rod *Lactobacillius acidophilus* bacteria that is found in the colon, intestines and vaginal areas.

ascending colon (*a-**send**-ng **kō**-lon*): Part of the large colon located between the transverse colon and the cecum. Found on the right side of the body, it extends from under the lower ribs and liver to the hip area.

averaging (***av**-er-jing*): Adding all the values and dividing by the number of values.

Axon Sea (***ax**-on sēz*): An axon is a long, slender projection of a nerve cell, or neuron, that transmits electrical currents/impulses away from the neuron's cell body; the author uses this term to refer to the cerebrospinal fluid (*sa-rē-**bro**-spīn-al fluid*), called the CSF, which is a clear, colorless fluid that occupies the subarachnoid (*sub-a-**rak**-noid*) space, the pia mater, and the ventricular system around and inside the brain and spinal cord; the brain and the spinal cord float in and are cushioned by the CSF.

bacterial colonies (*bak-**teer**-ē-al **kal**-ō-nēz*): A local population, group, or cluster of the same animal or plant; a colony of microscopic organisms growing on a surface of anything.

bad bacteria (*bak-**teer**-ē-a*): Bacteria that cause disease and sickness.

bad virus (***vī**-rus*): A virus that infects and causes disease and sickness.

barrel brandy alcohol: Rather than bury Admiral Lord Nelson at sea, sailors used barrel brandy alcohol to "embalm" (preserve) his body so they can take it to London to be properly honored.

Biff: Arthur's friend; short for *Bifidobacterium longum* (*bif-i-dō-**bak**-teer-ē-um **lon**-gum*); keeps digestion running smoothly.

Bladder Lake (***blad**-der lāk*): Urinary bladder; the hollow muscular and elastic organ that sits on the pelvic floor between the hips; urine enters the bladder by the ureters and leaves through the urethra (***yoor**-ēth-ra*).

blood color: The color of blood in the veins (deoxygenated blood) is maroon, not blue; blood in the arteries (oxygenated blood) becomes a brighter shade of maroon, not bright red; blood appears blue in the veins when viewing through skin and connective tissues; blood appears bright red outside of the body because it is fully exposed, not trapped within blood vessels; from Patty and Arthur's perspective inside Pembroke, venous blood (deoxygenated) is maroon colored and arterial blood (oxygenated) is brighter maroon.

blood capillaries (*blood **cap**-il-lar-ēz*): Tiny blood vessel connections between the arteries and veins where oxygen is brought to tissues and nutrients are transported from the digestive system to all parts of the body.

Brighter Maroon River: The name the author gives to the aorta (*ā-**or**-ta*), which is the largest single blood vessel in the body; in a human, it's approximately the diameter of an adult's thumb and carries oxygen-rich blood to all parts of the body through a system of small branching arteries, smaller arterioles, and tiny capillaries to all the tissues in the body.

bowels (***bow**-elz*): The intestines.

calculate (***cal**-kū-lāt*): To determine something mathematically, by reason, experience, and/or common sense.

camphor (***kam**-for*): White, volatile crystalline substance ($C_{10}H_{10}O_{16}$); aromatic essence of oils to sweeten the air, which were mixed with the barrel brandy alcohol for the "embalming" of Lord Nelson.

cancers (**kan**-sirs): Diseases caused by uncontrolled cell growth in any part of the body.

capsule (**cap**-sūl): A jellylike layer forming the outside layer of some bacteria.

carbohydrates (kar-bō-**hī**-drates): A group of chemical compounds found in food that contain sugars, starches, cellulose, water, and oxygen. Humans, mammals, and other animals and plants digest carbohydrates to produce energy.

Casey: Arthur's friend; short for Lactobacillus casei (lak-tō-bak-**sil**-lus **kay**-sē), helps good bacteria in the mouth and intestines.

cavity (**kav**-i-tē): An empty space, as in a body cavity; when cutting into Pembroke to remove the blockage in his bile duct, the veterinarian cut into Pembroke's abdominal cavity (ab-**do**-me-nal **kav**-i-tē).

cecum (**sē**-kum): Large open area (pouch-like) connecting the small and the large intestines.

Cecum Hollow (**sē**-kum **hal**-lō): The author's term for the pouch connecting the small and large intestines.

cell (*sell*): The smallest living unit of an individual plant, animal, or one-celled microorganism.

chemicals (**kem**-*ik-kals*): Combinations of elements that are found in plants, animals, and nonliving substances. Water is the combination of the elements hydrogen and oxygen. Salt is the combination of the elements sodium, chlorine, hydrogen, and oxygen. Muscle tissue is made up of many elements, including hydrogen, oxygen, calcium, magnesium, potassium, sodium, and chlorine.

chyme (*kīm*): Juicy, pulpy, digested food mass coming out of the stomach into the Twelve Finger/duodenal part of the small intestine.

cilia (**sil**-*ē-a*): Tiny hair or eyelash projections from cells along the esophagus that help keep food moving down to the stomach.

Circle of Willis (**sir**-*kl of* **wil**-*lis*): A circle of arteries located at the base of the brain that supply brighter maroon blood to the brain; named after Thomas Willis, an English physician (1621–1675).

circulatory system (**sir**-*qu-la-tor-ē* **sis**-*tem*): Also known as the blood-vascular (**vas**-*qu-lar*) system; composed of arteries that take the brighter maroon oxygenated blood from the heart through smaller and smaller arteries to capillaries where the oxygenated blood is distributed to all tissue; the veins collect the dark, murky maroon oxygen-depleted blood and take it back to the lungs for oxygenation. (Note: the only two exceptions are the pulmonary artery, which takes oxygen-depleted blood from the heart to the lungs, and the pulmonary vein, which takes oxygenated blood from the lungs to the heart.)

cloaking device (**klōk** *ng* **dē**-*vise*). Also called the protective shield; Patty has genetically inherited a survival "cloaking device" that hides her from animal defense mechanisms (leukocytes, T cells, white blood cells, antibodies, etc.), allowing her to travel throughout Pembroke without being killed. Although the "cloaking device" idea is fictional, it does have a scientific basis, as reported in Elisabeth Nadin's article "Viral Cloaking Device: How Viruses Evade the Immune System" in *Science Daily* (July 24, 2008) esciencenews.com/sources/science.daily/2008/07/18/viral.cloaking.device.how.viruses.evade.the.immune.system:

Viruses achieve their definition of success when they can thrive without killing their host. According to the CalTech article, biologists Pamela Bjorkman and Zhiru Yang of the California Institute of Technology have uncovered how one such virus, prevalent in humans, evolved over time to hide from the immune system.... The human immune system and the viruses hosted by our bodies are in a continual dance for survival—viruses ever seek new ways to evade detection, and our immune system devises new methods to hunt them down. Human Cytomegalovirus (HCMV), says Bjorkman, Caltech's Delbrück Professor of Biology and a Howard Hughes Medical Institute (HHMI) Investigator, "is the definition of a successful virus—it thrives but it doesn't affect the host."

collecting tube: Name given to the convoluted collecting tubule called the duct of Bellini that concentrates and transports urine from the nephrons to the renal pelvis.

colon wall (*cō-lon wall*): A long, hollow tube that runs from the cecum to the rectum and serves to remove water from digested food and let the remaining material, solid waste, move through it to the rectum, leaving the body through the anus.

Clomipramine *(klō-**mip**-re-mēn)*: An antidepressant medicated used to calm nervous behaviors in dogs and cats.

common carotid artery (***com**-mon **ka**-ra-ted **ar**-ter-ē*): An artery that supplies oxygenated blood (a brighter maroon color) to the head and neck; divides in the neck to form the external and internal carotid arteries.

common passageway: The term given by the author for the common bile duct (**com**-*mon bīl dukt*); the duct that the pancreas, gallbladder, and reddish-brown Hepatic Mountain/liver pour their bile and secretions into that goes into the Twelve Finger/duodenal part of the upper small intestine; also known as Twelve Fingers.

console (*kon-sōl*): To comfort someone in time of grief or disappointment.

constipated (*kon-***sti**-*pay-ted*): When the feces in the colon or rectum is slowed up, restricted from movement, and/or hardens.

Corazón River (*kor-a-***zōn** ri-ver): The name given by the author to all the blood pumped through the heart and the lungs as the oxygen-poor blood travels from the right atrium to the left ventricle through the pulmonary vein to the lungs back through the pulmonary vein to the right atrium through the left ventricle out into the Brighter Maroon River, the aorta (*ā-**or**-ta*). (Note: arteries usually carry brighter maroon oxygenated blood away from the heart with the exception of the pulmonary artery that carries maroon oxygen-poor blood away from the heart to the lungs; likewise, veins usually carry oxygen-poor blood to the heart with the exception of the pulmonary vein that carries brighter maroon oxygenated blood to the heart.)

curiosity (*kur-ē-os-i-tē*): The strong need or desire to know or learn something.

cystic duct (*sis-tik dukt*): A short duct leading to the gallbladder from the common bile duct.

cytoplasm (*sī-tō-plasm*): Colorless liquid material within a living cell, excluding the nucleus.

dangerous (*dān-jer-us*): Likely to cause harm, injury, and/or death.

demandingly (*dē-man-ding-lē*): The way one insists, demands, dictates, or commands what they want to be done.

denature (*dē-nay-chur*): To take away or alter the natural qualities of a cell; denaturing is the process of causing proteins to lose their shapes/structures by applying external stress—such as placing them in strong acids, bases, or solvents (alcohol chloroform) or heating them at or above 100 degrees Centigrade (212 degrees Fahrenheit)—killing the cells, bacteria, viruses, or enzymes in the process.

descending colon (*dē-send-ng kō-lon*): Part of the large colon located between the sigmoid located near the left hip side of the body and the transverse colon just under the ribs on the left side of the body.

destination (*des-te-nā-shun*): Place, location, or stop.

diarrhea (*dĭ-a-rhē-a*): Condition that turns waste in the intestines to liquid.

digestive system (*dĭ-jes-tiv sis tem*): In humans, dogs, cats, and some other animals, an internal tube/tract that mechanically and chemically breaks down food to be taken into the bloodstream and distributed to all parts of the body.

DNA: Stands for Deoxyribonucleic Acid (*dē-ox-ē-rī-bō-nū-klē-ic a-sid*); a group of chemical compounds that carries genetic information for how living things reproduce themselves; DNA of an enzyme tells the enzyme how to produce more enzymes that are just like the parent enzymes.

dormant (*dor-mant*): Inactive, asleep, resting, inert.

ducts: Pipes or tubes carrying stuff to different parts of the body: liver bile, sweat gland ducts, lobar ducts, mucous ducts, tear ducts; some glands—endocrine glands—don't have ducts and secrete substances directly into the bloodstream.

duodenal curve (*du-od-**de**-nel curv*): The first 10 to 12 inches of the duodenum; the first part of the small intestines just under the stomach that is curved.

duodenum (*du-**od**-de-nem*): The first 10 to 12 inch section of small intestine, below the stomach; also called Twelve Fingers.

eliminated (*ē-**lim**-i-nā-ted*): To remove completely.

embarrassed (***em**-bair-ast*): Caused to feel awkward, self-conscious, or ashamed.

endangered (***en**-dăn-jurd*): To put someone or something in harm's way, in a dangerous place.

energy (***en**-er-jē*): The forces, resources, capacity, and capability to do work.

entrée (***ahn**-tray*): The main course of a meal.

enzyme (***en**-zīm*): Proteins produced by different glands and organs in the body that can increase the rate of a chemical reaction in the body without being consumed by the reaction catalyst (***cat**-i-list*); can use other energy sources around them (free energy or ΔG) for a chemical reactions; can provide the starting energy for the chemical reactions they make; and can use available energy around them (free energy) to make the reaction go faster.

enzyme disorders at Pirate's Cove: Patty and Arthur run into enzymes running wild inside Pembroke's pancreas, posing life-threatening consequences. The tactic they use to defeat the pancreatic pirate enzymes is fictionalized, but it has roots in current scientific research. The article "Disrupt an Enzyme, Destroy Drug-Resistant Superbugs," by Nikhil Swaminathan (*Scientific American*, July 10, 2007/ scientificamerican. com/article.cfm?id=disrupt-an-enzyme-destroy-resistant-bugs) presents the same concept that Patty is telling Arthur about to disable Pembroke's pancreatic enzymes that are running wild:

In the continuing battle to counter growing antibiotic resistance, a new finding may help keep our current arsenal of antibacterial agents from having to be scrapped and replaced by an as yet unrealized new infection-fighting therapy. By targeting an enzyme that bacteria use to swap genetic material, researchers at the University of North Carolina at Chapel Hill, have stopped the microbes' ability to spread, among other advantageous mutations, resistance to antibiotics.

"It turns out bacteria are very social," says Matthew Redinbo, a UNC associate professor of chemistry, biochemistry, and biophysics. "They pass genes between one another that keep one another intact." He adds that this transfer can occur between bacteria of either the same or different species.

esophagus *(e-**sof**-a-gus)*: A muscular tube extending from the mouth to the stomach filled with mucus, which makes the food slide easier to the stomach.

excrement *(**eks**-cre-ment)*: Waste matter discharged from a living plant, animal, or microorganism; feces, poop, poo.

exhilarated *(egg-**zill**-er-rate-ted)*: Excited, elated, delighted, vibrant, thrilled, energized, etc.

extinguished *(ex-**ting**-gwisht)*: To stop or cease existing.

famished *(**fam**-isht)*: Extremely hungry.

fats: Naturally oily or greasy substance deposited in animals under skin and around some organs.

feces *(**fē**-cēs)*: Fecal matter or poop.

fermentation *(**fer**-men-**tā**-shon)*: The chemical breakdown of substances by bacteria, yeast, or other microorganisms as in digesting food, souring milk, and making grapes into wine.

First Street Caudal Station (*first street **ka**-dal **stā**-shun*): Name author gives to the first segment of the caudal bone closest to South Port.

floral bacteria (***floor**-al bak-**ter**-ē-a*): Name given bacteria living in/around the digestive system.

floral bacterial colonies: Areas where probiotics (good bacteria) grow; bacteria "towns."

flu (*floo*): Short for influenza (*in-**floo**-en-za*); A virus, sometimes fatal, causing fever, sore throat, muscle pains, bad headaches, coughing, weakness, and all over discomfort in persons or animals infected.

front brain: Also called the telencephalon (*tel-en-**sef**-a-lon*), it contains the cerebrum (***ser**-rē-brum*); located in the front of the head, the part of the brain that thinks, plans, and directs voluntary behavior.

fruit bacteria (*bak-**te**-rē-a*): Bacteria, molds, and yeasts live on the surface of fruits, which is why fruits should be washed before they are eaten.

gallbladder *(gal-**blad**-dur)*: The storage area or bladder for liver bile, which is used to breakdown fatty foods, which helps digestion.

gawking *(**gaw**-king)*: Looking in amazement, gaping, and staring with mouth wide-open; ogling, gazing.

gene *(jēn)*: A gene is biological *(bī-ō-**la**-je-cal)* material in a living organism (a single cell or multiple cell plant or animal, including humans) that passes on the mental and/or physical traits of parent cells to the parent's offspring.

genetic transformation *(**je**-ne-tic trans-for-**mā**-shun)*: The process of changing genetic material that changes the mental and/or physical traits of living organisms and their offspring.

good bacteria *(bak-**te**-rē-a)*: Bacteria in the intestines that help digestion, also known as probiotics.

good virus *(**vī**-rus)*: A virus that helps one stay healthy.

gray convolution *(grey con-ve-**loo**-shun)*: A coiling or rolling of the brain; gray matter refers to dark tissue of the brain and spinal cord.

Great Brown River: The name given by the author to the

fecal (*fē-kal*) matter that is flowing through Pembroke's lower digestive system (the intestines and colon).

Great Maroon River: The name given by the author to the superior vena cava (*su-pe-rē-or ve-na ka-va*), which is the largest vein carrying oxygen-poor blood back to the right atrium (*ā-trē-um*) of the heart.

gyrations (*jī-rā-shons*): Hands and/or other things wildly dancing, moving in circles and spirals.

Hepatic Mountain (*he-pat-ik moun-ten*): The name given by the author to refer to the liver, a huge organ that rids the body of toxins and poisons; the largest gland in the body, weighing three pounds and as large as a football; it is set on the right side of the abdomen under the lower ribs in between the intestine and heart; it is indispensable to life.

historical footnote (*his-tōr-ik-al foot-nōt*): In a history book, interesting facts are sometimes put at the bottom of the page (footnotes) for the reader to read if he or she wants.

history (*his-tor-rē*): Study of past events.

host (*hōst*): Organism like a single cell plants or animals or protozoan *(prō-**te**-zō-an)* that a parasite *(**par**-a-sīt)* lives on, feeding off the plant or animal.

hydrochloric acid *(hī-dro-**klo**-rik **a**-sid)*: A strong solution of hydrogen chloride *(hī-**dro**-jen **klo**-rīd)* water found in the stomachs of animals that aids in the digestion of foods.

hysteria *(hiss-**tare**-rē-ah)*: Stress produced uncontrollable excitement or emotion, overdramatic behavior, panic, fit of madness.

immune reserves: *(**em**-mūn **rē**-zervs)*: When more antibodies, T cells, white blood cells, and NK cells are needed, the immune system calls up the reserves.

immune system *(**em**-mūn **sis**-tem)*: Our organ police and reserve antibodies that fight viral, bacterial, fungal, and other infections and toxic or foreign invasions of the body and organs; our skin protection, our antibodies, T cells, white blood cells, mesenchymal *(mes-in-**kī**-mal)* and lymphocyte *(**lim**-fo-site)* systems; defense system that helps prevent the spread of bacteria, viruses, and/or toxins in the body.

impressed *(**im**-prest)*: Made someone feel respect/reverence; made an imprint on them.

infect (*in-fekt*): Person, organism, or cell that causes illness, disease, and/or death of another life.

instinctively (*in-stink-tiv-lē*): Natural, inborn: survival instinct.

internal carotid arteries (*in-ter-nal ka-ra-ted ar-ter-ēz*): The major arteries that supply blood to the brain; divides in the brain into the anterior cerebral artery and the middle cerebral artery.

intestines (*in-tes-tines*): General name given to the small intestine, colon, and rectum.

Islands of Langerhans (*ī-lands of lan-ger-hans*): Located inside the pancreas; functions are many: 1) manufacturing alpha cells that produce glucagons to raise blood pressure levels; beta cells that produce insulin and amylin to control the metabolism (chemical reactions) breaking down sugars, starches, and fats in the body; delta cells that produce somatostatin, which is a growth hormone or growth inhibiting hormone that affects many organs: stomach, liver, brain, etc.; PP cells that produce a pancreatic polypeptide that regulates activities in the pancreas; and epsilon cells that produce ghrelin, which stimulates hunger.

kayak (*kī-yak*): A type of canoe commonly used to

travel streams, lakes, rivers, bays and estuaries, and the oceans.

kidneys (**kid**-*nēs*): The organs that filter blood wastes, maintain acid-base balance, regulate blood pressure, and produce hormones, including calcitriol (**kal**-*si-trol*), renin (**rē**-*nin*), and erthropoietin (*e-rith-thrō*-**poy**-*e-tin*); allow extra fluids/wastes to pass through the ureters and out of the body in the form of urine.

lag phase (*lag fāz*): Term given to the time it takes for new bacteria to recover from the shock of being in a new place, to make new enzymes needed to metabolize, and to grow in size. No binary fission happens during a bacterium's lag phase. The next phase, the log phase, is when a bacterium's reproduction happens at a very fast rate. The phase after that is called the stationary phase, when growth cannot continue because the bacteria colony is limited by lack of food for the bacteria or lack of space for the bacteria to grow. The final phase is called the death phase. All living things have a life cycle (e.g., human life cycle: infanthood, childhood, adulthood, and death; bacteria have a lag phase, log phase, stationary phase, and death phase).

large intestine (*larj in*-**tes**-*ten*): The entire length of the digestive tube that runs from the cecum to the rectum and includes the ascending colon, transverse colon, descending colon, and the sigmoid, illiac, and pelvic colons.

left atrium (*left $\bar{a}$-trē-um*): Upper space/chamber of the heart receiving oxygen-rich blood (a brighter maroon colored blood) from the lungs through the pulmonary artery pumping the blood through the mitral valve (***mī**-tral valv*) into the left ventricle.

left ventricle (*left **ven**-trik-el*): The lower space/chamber of the heart that receives oxygenated blood (a brighter maroon colored blood) and pumps it through the aortic valve into the aorta, which carries oxygenated blood throughout the body, including the coronary arteries of the heart.

legion (***lē**-jun*): In ancient Roman times, a legion was an army of between three and six thousand soldiers.

liquid or water vapor (***lik**-quid **vā**-por*): A vapor is a substance that at a certain temperature is a gas, at a lower temperature turns from a vapor into a liquid, and at a still lower temperature turns from a vapor into a solid.

liver (***li**-ver*): A large organ located on the right side of the body that has many functions: stores sugar, removes toxins from the blood, produces hormones that regulate growth, disposes of old blood cells, as well as creating bile that helps in the digestion of fats in foods.

liver bend (*li-ver bend*): The turn of the transverse colon that is next to the liver.

liver bile (*li-ver bīl*): A dark green to yellowish brown salty fluid made in the liver that helps digest fats in food.

maneuvers (*ma-new-vers*): To expertly move or do a number of moves skillfully; Patty knows the area outside of the main digestive system; the path she is taking goes through the Sphincter of Oddi into the common duct that leads past the pancreatic duct, and then through the duct to the gallbladder to the hepatic duct to the liver (also known as Hepatic Mountain).

Maroon Lake: The name the author gives to the *cavernous sinus (ca-ver-us sī-nus),* which is a large pool of veins inside the brain that collects deoxygenated blood (a dark, murky reddish colored blood) from the brain and takes it back to the heart through a system of veins.

medial sacral artery (*mē-dĕl sak-kril ar-ter-ē*): A small artery from the descending aorta. The medial sacral artery has small branches that pass on to the end portion of the rectum.

ménages (*me-nen-jēz*): The three-layer covering of the brain and spinal system: the dura mater (outside covering of the ménages), the arachnoid mater (middle layer of the ménages), and the pia mater (the innermost layer of the ménages).

microbe (*mīkrōb*): Name for a microorganism (bacterium, virus, or germ) that causes disease or fermentation.

microinch (*mī-kro-inch*): One millionth of an inch.

microvilli (*mī-krō-vil-lī*): Many, many microscopic lobes or fingerlike projections coming from the entire surface of the inside of the intestines and colon that allow digested nutrients to be absorbed into the body.

middle brain: Name for diencephalon (*die-en-sef-ah-lon*) that controls chewing, directs neural impulses, maintains equilibrium, controls eye movement, maintains vision, translates facial sensation, maintains hearing, produces saliva, controls swallowing, and activates respiration, smell, and taste.

minerals (*min-er-als*): A mixture from nonliving matter that helps cell growth.

modified virus (**mod**-i-fīd *vī-rus*): Gene modification that involves the insertion or deletion of genes; when genes are inserted, they usually come from a different species (Arthur the bacterium in the case of this story), which is called horizontal gene transfer; Patty horizontally transfers some of Arthur's genetic material to modify her genetic material and fight Pembroke's pituitary cancer; in *Pembroke*, what Patty Virus did is theoretically possible, but fictitious (see the *Pituitary Cancer* definition, which gives more information about this subject).

mouth and teeth: Food is held in the mouth and mechanically broken down by the teeth.

Mrs. Lactose (**lak**-*toz*): A teacher's name in story, which is based on the name given sugar that is in milk.

myrrh (*mer*): Dried oil gum secretion of commiphora/dhidin trees; Egyptians used myrrh as the main ingredient to embalm mummies.

natural environment (**na**-*cher-al en-vī-ron-ment*): All living and nonliving things on Earth.

Nelson Virus (**nel**-*son vī-rus*): A virus based on scientific research summarized in "A few good viruses" by Hamish

Clarke (*Cosmos*, February 2007, www.cosmosmagazine. com/node/1024):

Pavel Osten from Northwestern University in Chicago, Illinois, recently co-authored a paper on the use of viruses as DNA delivery systems, or vectors. "In my view, it is most likely that this work [gene therapy] will become a mainstream treatment of some of the devastating brain disorders for which there is currently no treatment," he wrote.

> nephron (*nef-ron*): The basic unit in the kidney that filters out and changes urea into urine for removal from the body; reabsorbs what is needed and excretes the rest.

nervous system (*nerv-us sis-tem*): Network of nerve cells and fibers that carry nerve impulses throughout the body (autonomic nervous system, central nervous system, peripheral nervous system).

neurons (*ner-ons*): A nerve cell that is electrically excitable that transmits information by electrical and chemical signals.

next tiny artery: The middle cerebral artery (*mid-dal sir-rē-bral ar-ter-ē*); one of three paired arteries carrying brighter maroon blood to the cerebrum.

NK cells: Natural killer cells that the immune system sends out to kill bad cells and engulf foreign objects in the body.

nutrients (*nū-trē-ents*): Anything that provides food that is good for growth, health, and good condition.

old puppy brain: Author's term for the medulla oblongata (*me-dul-la ob-lon-ga-ta*), or simply medulla; the lower half of the brain stem, which contains the centers for automatically controlling heart rate, blood pressure, breathing, and involuntary muscle responses.

one million times his age: Arthur has divided or reproduced 8 times and is going on his ninth cell division; Patty has infected other cells and has divided or reproduced 8,000,000 times; the time it takes for a virus or bacterium to divide varies; for the purposes of this story, a virus and bacterium or the combination of a virus-bacterium division takes twenty minutes.

organism (*or-gan-izm*): An individual plant, animal, or other living form.

other systems: Skeletal system, joints and ligaments system, muscular and fascia system, blood-vascular system, lymphatic system, peripheral nervous system, respiratory system, digestive system, urogenital system (also known as the reproductive system), endocrine system, and the immune system.

pancreatic bile *(pan-**krē**-a-tik bĭl)*: The chemicals manufactured in the pancreas that empty through the pancreatic duct into the top part of the small intestine, called the duodenum or Twelve Fingers, which is the 10- to 12-inch section of small intestine located below the stomach.

pancreatic duct *(pan-**krē**-a-tik dukt)*: A passageway or tube transporting pancreatic bile to the common passageway, also called the common bile duct, on its way to the upper intestines (duodenum or Twelve Fingers) through the Sphincter of Oddi.

Pancreatic Seas *(pan-**krē**-a-tik sēz)*: The name the author gives to the small amounts of tissue fluid in the pancreas that the pirates use in the story to get from island to island, giving them passage to any tissue in the body so they could digest whatever they wanted to digest.

pancreatic tail *(pan-**krē**-a-tik tail)*: The pancreas has five parts: uncinate, head, neck, body, and tail.

pancreatitis *(pan-crē-a-**tī**-tis)*: The reaction of the pancreatic tissue due to injury or irritation producing pain, swelling, redness, and heat; can be caused by certain drugs, infections, or very high levels of alcohol or fats in bloodstream.

parasite (*par-a-sīt*): An organism that lives on another organism (its host) and benefits from feeding off the host.

part of the puppy brain too: Actually the metencephalon (*me-ten-sef-a-lon*) is made up of the pons (*pons*) and the cerebellum (*ser-ra-bel-lum*) and developed from the hindbrain or medulla; the pons regulates breathing; the cerebellum works to coordinate muscle movements, maintain posture, and integrate sensory information from the inner ear and proprioceptors (*pro-prē-o-sep-tors*), sensors deep in muscle, heart, and joint tissues.

Parvovirus (*par-vō-vī-rus*): Infects animals like dogs, contagious, often fatal, attacks heart muscles.

Patty Virus (*pat-tē vī-rus*): One of the main characters in the story.

Pembroke's immune system (*em-mūn sis-tem*): A standing reserve of T cells, antibodies, NK cells, and lymphocytes (*lim-fō-sites*) or white blood cells that attack viruses, parasites, and bacteria invading Pembroke and disable foreign objects that penetrate Pembroke.

Pembroke's thorax (**Pem**-*brook's* **tho**-*rax*): The division of Pembroke's body that contains the heart and lungs and everything lying between his head and abdomen; also known as the thoracic cavity (*tho*-**ras**-*ik* **ca**-*va-tē*).

penetrate (**pen**-*e-trāt*): To force something inside or through something else; the bullet penetrates the armor or the tunnel penetrated the earth's core.

Pentothal (**pen**-*tuh-thawl*): Brand name for thiopental sodium, which is used to cause drowsiness or sleep before surgery.

perfected over millions of years: Refers to the "cloaking device" evolved in Nelson Viruses.

perish (**pe**-*rish*): To die.

pharynx (**fari**-*nks*): Cavity behind nose and mouth, which aids in sending food to the esophagus.

pincher movement (**pin**-*chur* **mov**-*ment*): Flanks (sides) of the enemy are attacked simultaneously in a pinching motion by opposition forces that have drawn the enemy in and surrounded them.

Pirate's Cove: The name Patty gives to a possibly fatal condition where something goes wrong with the Islands of Langerhans that allows the digestive enzymes to be released into the pancreas and begin digesting the pancreas; this condition causes inflammation of the pancreas, swelling, loss of function, and bleeding, as the enzymes get into the bloodstream and get passed on throughout the entire body; pancreatic enzymes leak out into the abdominal cavity and do severe damage; the pirates are the out-of-control enzymes.

> pituitary cancer (*pe-**too**-e-ter-ē**can**-sir*): Most pituitary growths in dogs are not cancers, but they still can produce serious effects as they grow and are rarely curable. In Pembroke's case, the pituitary tumor is cancerous, having life-threatening consequences. Although the condition is fictional, there is a scientific base supporting the way Patty Virus and Arthur Bacterium attack the cancer: "Modified viruses can destroy cancer cells" Dr. John Chester, published by Guardian. co.uk (April 22, 2010) (also see, *Gene Therapy*, 2010, original article Guardian. co.uk/ www.nhs.uk/news/2010/04April/ Pages/virus-targets-kills-cancer-cells.aspx "Retargeted adenoviral cancer gene therapy for tumor cells over expressing epidermal growth factor receptor or urokinase-type plasminogen activator receptor" by T. J. Harvey, D. Burdon, L. Steele, N. Ingram,

G. D. Hall, P. J. Selby, R. G. Vile, P. A. Cooper, S. D. Shnyder, and J. D. Chester): Viruses can be modified to seek out and destroy cancer cells, scientists said today. Laboratory tests at Leeds University have shown how proteins can be added to a virus to enable it to recognise unique markers on the surface of tumours … Now the researchers are hoping to move from the laboratory and begin human testing. Dr. John Chester, who led the Cancer Research UK-funded study, published in *Gene Therapy*, said the modified viruses deliver genes, which could make cancer cells more sensitive to drugs. Dr. Lesley Walker, from Cancer Research UK, said: "This exciting early laboratory work points to a new way of attacking cancer cells by targeting the unique markers on cancer cells. It could have real benefits for patients, with treatments tailored to their cancer, but we first have to test it through clinical trials … This approach could be a step forward for gene therapy, particularly as it is quicker, easier, and cheaper to mix and match the targeting proteins rather than engineer a completely new gene therapy virus," Dr. Walker continued.

pituitary gland (*pe-**too**-e-tar-ē gland*): Also called the master gland, because it produces hormones (***hor-mones***) that control other glands and many body functions; has two parts, the front, or anterior pituitary (*an-**teer**-ē-or pe-**too**-e-tar-ē*), and the back part, the posterior pituitary (*pos-**teer**-ē-or pe-**too**-e-tar-ē*); Arthur and Patty adventures focused on the anterior pituitary, which regulates/controls growth, sexual development, skin pigmentation, thyroid function, and adrenocortical (*ad-**drē**-no-**cor**-tik-kal*) function, and which pumps adrenalin (*a-**dren**-a-lin*) into humans and animals to respond to stress.

poisons (***poi***-*zens*): Anything eaten or absorbed into the body that causes death or injury.

pollute (***pol***-*lūt*): To spoil, taint, or infect the natural environment, including Pembroke.

Polly: Arthur's friend; short for *Bacterial polysaccharides* (*bak-**teer**-ee-ahl pol-ee-**sak**-er-rides*), which survive in harsh environments.

polypeptides (*pol-ē-**pep**-tīdz*): Chains of molecules of hydrogen (H) and oxygen (O) connected by cells that help cells function.

protective shield (*pro-**tek**-tiv sh*ē*ld*): Another name for Patty's cloaking device.

proteins (***prō***-*t*ē*ns*): Large molecules of nitrogen-rich living matter that builds muscles.

pyloric sphincter (***p*ī**-*lor-rik* **sfink**-*ter*): The ring muscle at the bottom of the stomach that controls the amount of chyme released by the stomach into the upper small intestine.

rectum (***rek***-*tum*): Storage unit for food wastes.

renal artery (***r*ē**-*nal* ***ar***-*ter-*ē*): Branches off the aorta and carries oxygenated blood (a brighter maroon colored blood) to the kidneys; renal refers to the kidneys or the kidney area.

Renal Falls (***r*ē**-*nal falls*): The name the author gives to the renal pelvis (**pel**-vis) area, which collects all the watery wastes from the minor calyax (***ka***-*laks*) and major calyax and the ureter (***ūr***-*r*ē*-ter*) that channels the watery waste down to the urinary bladder (***yr***-*en-ary* ***blad***-*der*).

reproductive systems (*r*ē*-pr*ō*-**duk**-tiv* **sis**-*tems*): Makes copies by sexual reproduction; simpler forms of life, such as bacteria, reproduce themselves by splitting in half over and over again; viruses have no reproductive systems and have to use the bodies of other cells, including bacteria, to reproduce themselves through infecting them.

retreat (*rē-trēt*): To move back or withdraw to a safe place.

ribosomes (*rī-bō-zōmz*): Ribosomes give cytoplasm in bacteria a granular look under an electron microscope; cytoplasm granules are thought to put polypeptides and proteins together to make genetic messages.

right atrium (*rīt ā-trē-um*): The first space or chamber of the heart that receives blood from the superior and inferior venae cavae (plural of vena cava) through the tricuspid valve (*trī-cus-pid valv*); the tricuspid valve stops the blood from going back into the venae cavae (*vēn-a ca-va*) and, when the right atrium contracts, forces the deoxygenated blood into the right ventricle (*rīt ven-trik-el*).

right ventricle (*rīt ven-trik-el*): The lower chamber/space in the heart that receives oxygen-depleted blood from the right atrium and pumps it through the pulmonary valve (*pul-mo-nar-ē valv*) through the pulmonary artery into the lung.

Rimadyl (***rim**-a-dill*): An anti-inflammatory medicine that works on a dog's arthritic joints and muscle pain, allowing for more comfortable movement; side effects may include loss of appetite, vomiting, diarrhea, loss of muscle control, and jaundice.

rudeness (***rood**-nes*): Offensive, impolite, or ill-mannered.

Sal: Arthur's friend; short for *Lactobacillus salivarius* (*lak-tō-bak **sil**-lus sa-li-**ver**-ē-us*; probiotic (*prō-bī-o-tik*) to help prevent infections.

saline solution (***sā**-lēn sō-**loo**-shon*): A water and salt mixture that is sterile (***ster**-il*), meaning it is free from bacteria and other living microorganisms.

saliva (***sa**-lī-va*): A watery substance filled with enzymes to help digestion that is produced in the mouth by salivary glands under the tongue; moistens food so it slides down to the stomach easier.

salivary glands (***sal**-li-vair-ē*): Glands under the tongue that produce saliva. Food taken into the mouth is mixed with the saliva and chemically broken down to help digestion.

sarcastic (*sar-**kas**-tik*): A sharp, bitter use of words that usually mean just the opposite of what the normal words mean; example: "That's one of the most intelligent comments I've heard from you today, Jeff."

scalpel (**skal**-*pel*): A surgeon's knife.

scientist (**sī**-*en-tist*): Person who is learning/has great knowledge about the natural universe.

S-curve: The shape of an S, or sigmoid (**sig**-*moid*).

seizure (**sē**-*jur*): A sudden attack of illness; can be caused by a stroke, an epileptic fit, or a brain aneurysms breaking.

Serous Sea (**se**-*rus see*): The name the author gives to serous fluids; straw-colored, transparent fluids that allow the intestines and other body organs to smoothly move in the abdominal cavity; serous fluids are also found in the bloodstream and other parts of the body.

sheepish: A facial look/expression that shows embarrassment, shame, or lack of worth.

shock (*shok*): A dangerous medical condition indicating a fall in blood pressure caused by loss of blood, severe burns, bacterial/viral infections, body organs shutting down, allergic reactions, sever and sudden emotional distress, snake bites, or toxins that could lead to death; symptoms are cold and/or pallid skin, rapid pulse, irregular breathing, dilated pupils; shock is a life-threatening condition that happens when the body is not getting enough blood flow.

sigmoid bend (**sig**-*moid bend*): The turn from the rectum to the descending colon.

slaughter (**slaw**-*ter*): The killing of a large number of living things: bacteria, viruses, animals, or large numbers of any living things.

small intestines (*small* **in**-*tes-tens*): The intestines run between the stomach and colon; a mixture of bile and food make a liquid *chyme* that comes into contact with small blood vessels that carry nutrients—vitamins, minerals, fats, sugars, water—to all parts of the body from the small intestines; the small intestines measure about 22 feet in humans and 11 feet in a Pembroke Welsh Corgi, like Pembroke.

smooth muscles: Muscles around the small and large intestines and rectum (bowels) that automatically squeeze, pushing the waste along inside the digestive system.

sphenoid bone (**sfē**-*noid bōn*): A compound bone that is

part of the bony base of the brain behind the eye and below the front part of the brain; has two broad "wings" from its sides and contains two air-filled sinuses—the ones that hurt between the eyes sometime when people have sinus infections.

sphincter muscle (**sfink**-*ter* **mus**-*sel*): A sphincter is a round or ring-shaped muscle that controls the flow of bile from the liver, bile from the pancreas, chyme from the stomach, and so on.

Sphincter of Oddi (**sfink**-*ter of* **ō**-*dee*): The round muscle at the end of the pancreatic duct that controls the flow of bile from the pancreas, liver, and gallbladder into Twelve Fingers in the small intestine.

spiderweb: The second layer of the ménages called the arachnoid mater (**a**-*rak*-*noid* **ma**-*ter*); literally the "spider mother."

spirits of wine: An old name for alcohol.

spleen (*splēn*): Body organ that cleans the bloodstream; part of the immune system.

spleen turn: The turn of the transverse colon that is next to the spleen.

splenic artery (**splin**-ik **ar**-ter-e): The splenic artery, formerly called the lienal (**lē**-nal) artery, runs along and branches into the pancreas on its way to the spleen.

stained glass windows: Colored glass used to form pictures in windows and doors.

stomach (**stom**-ak): Also called Acid Lake by the author; pear-shaped organ between the esophagus and the small intestine where chewed food mixed with saliva is broken down by acid, making chyme; food is mixed with acid and enzymes and made into liquid *chyme*.

stopped-up colon (**Kō**-lon): Poop or fecal matter in the colon is somehow restricted or slowed or hardened enough to stop the flow of poop.

strain (strāin): A type, kind, or breed of animal or plant.

sugars (**su**-gars): Sweet-tasting crystals, which the body turns into energy.

surgery (**sir**-jer-ē): Treatment of disease or injury by cutting into the body to make repairs.

swine flu: A virus pigs get that does not often infect humans; the virus is killed in well-cooked pig meat.

symbiosis *(sim-bī-**ō**-sis)*: Interaction between two different organisms living in close physical association that benefits each organism; an example is clown fish living in the tentacles of sea anemone.

T cells: The "T" stands for thymus, a specialize organ in the throat area that produces T cells, which are important cells in the immune system.

tender mother: The pia mater *(pēa **ma**-ter)*; literally the "tender mother" that is the innermost layer of the ménages.

Thyroid Station *(**thī**-roid **stā**-shon)*: The name the author gives to one of the largest endocrine glands in the body, the thyroid, which is located in the neck below the thyroid cartilage (Adam's apple); the thyroid controls how quickly the body uses energy and makes proteins, and it controls how the body reacts to hormones.

tiny filters: The name author gives to the kidney's nephrons *(**neh**-frons)*, which purify and filter the blood of waste.

tissue *(**tish**-shoo)*: All parts of the body are made up of tissue; animals have muscle tissue, connective tissue, epithelial tissue, nerve tissue, pancreatic tissue, liver tissue, etc.; plants have meristematic tissue, epidermis and cork tissue, parenchyma tissue, etc.

torso (*tor*-sō): The trunk of the body, without head, arms, and legs.

tough part: The dura mater (*du*-ra *ma*-ter); literally the "tough mother" that is the first layer of the ménages.

toxin (*toks*-in): Poison produced by or comes from a microorganism (virus, bacteria) that causes death or injury or genetic change; also antigenic poisons produced by plants and animals that trigger immune system responses.

trachea (*tray*-kē-a): The windpipe; the connection between the mouth and the lungs.

Trafalgar (*tra*-fal-gar): The cape of Trafalgar is on the south coast of Spain and was the site of the sea battle between England and the combined fleets of Spain and France; under the leadership of Admiral Horatio Nelson, who was killed in the battle, the Spanish and French warships were defeated, stopping the Napoleonic invasion of England on October 21, 1805.

tranquilizer (*tran*-kwi-līz-er): A drug that reduces tension or anxiety.

transformation of enzymes *(trans-for-**mā**-shon ov **en**-zīmz)*: To make a dramatic change in appearance, character, or dramatically change in some other way the essence of a life-form or thing.

transverse colon *(**trans**-verse **kō**-lon)*: Middle part of the colon, passing right to left below the stomach.

traverse *(**tra**-verse)*: To travel or journey over/across; pass over, wander, and roam.

tubules *(**toob**-byools)*: Small tube structures in the kidney that filter blood and produce urine.

Turkish Saddle: Also known as the Stella Turcica *(**stel**-la **tur**-se-kah)* a saddle-shaped bone covered by the ménages that holds the pituitary gland inside the middle of the brain.

tweezers *(**twee**-zers)*: Small instruments shaped like pinchers for picking up small objects.

Twelve Fingers: The name given by the author for the duodenum *(do-**od**-deh-nem)*; the first section of the small intestine in humans, dogs, cats, and other higher vertebrates; the 10- to 12-inch section of small intestine below the stomach.

upper thyroid artery (**up**-*per* **thī**-*roid* **ar**-*ter-ē*): A branch of the common carotid artery that goes to the thyroid.

urea (**ur**-*ē-a*): A substance with the chemical formula $CO(NH_2)_2$; a strong smelling ammonia that, if found in large amounts, will lead to kidney dysfunction; urea is turned into urine by the kidneys; blood nitrogen tests (BUN) are used to measure the amount of urea nitrogen in the blood; high urea or ammonia levels left untreated can cause the "brain and spinal cord to swell, causing irreversible brain damage, seizures, coma, and death" (Wellness.com: Urea Cycle Disorders).

Urine River (**ūr**-*in* **ri**-*ver*): The name the author gives to urine flowing through the ureter to the bladder; contains liquid, watery, soluble wastes from the bloodstream and excess water, sugar, and other compounds not needed by the body.

vague (*vāg*): Unclear, hazy, fuzzy.

valves (*valvs*): Any of the small cusps or flaps or "gates" that seal and prevent the venous blood from flowing backward.

veterinarian (*ve-ter-i-***nar***-ē-an*): An animal doctor; a qualified person that treats sick and injured animals. Also called a vet, which is short for veterinarian.

villi (***vill**-ĭ*): Larger than microvilli, villi are microscopic lobes or fingerlike projections coming from the entire surface of the inside of the intestines and colon that allow digested nutrients to be absorbed into the body.

virology (*vĭ-**rol**-ō-jē*): The scientific study of viruses.

virus (***vĭ**-rus*): A tiny infecting organism, too tiny to be seen by a regular microscope, that infects living cells and uses them to reproduce more viruses, digest and absorb food, and produce energy.

vitamins (***vĭ**-ta-mins*): B1, B2, B3, B5, and B11; release food energy; promote healthy skin, eye surface, gums, and hair; a mixture from living matter that helps cell growth.

West Nile virus: A virus that was first identified in Africa that infects humans and mammals through mosquito bites.

white cells: Also called leukocytes (***lew**-kō-sites*); cells of the immune system that defend the body against infectious diseases and foreign materials.

whoop-de-do: Lively noise, fuss, debate, merrymaking.

MORE ABOUT THE AUTHOR

IN 1961, Taylor Samuel Lyen began his educational career as a sixth-grade teacher in a self-contained classroom at Sydney Elementary School in the Castro Valley Unified School District. A true science lover, Mr. Lyen taught reading, literature, poetry, arithmetic, social sciences, English, and writing with biological sciences at the core of his classroom curriculum. He also taught the principles of law, setting up a student court when he became principal of Sydney School in 1970. As the principal of Palomares Elementary School, he supported Mrs. Marge Galvin's dream to make the school an environmental science model for the district. He developed partnerships with the Berkeley Academy of Sciences and Lawrence Livermore National Laboratory to bring field scientists into the schools to support classroom teachers in creating science classroom experiences, placing children in the role of real research science associates. In the mid-1980s, as an assistant superintendent of instruction, he wrote grants and developed partnerships between Castro Valley High School and the scientists at Lawrence Livermore National Laboratory to further science education for teachers and students. From 1998 through 2000, he wrote grants for the school district, supporting science and mathematics education. In 2001, Taylor retired from the school district after forty years of public service. Today, he resides in San Francisco to be with his son and his son's family and lives in Gold River to be with his daughter's family and his grandchildren. His time is spent writing books, golfing, and volunteering for a variety of community organizations.

OTHER BOOKS

Alma's Journey (2011)

Oxbowl Incident:
A Case for Jesus Christ through Scientific Inquiry
(2010)

Life Ain't All Kitties and Bunnies (2007)

Thanks for the Share … Thanks for the Chair (2007)

Mischievous Rascal: Breaking the Seventh Seal (2005)

Student Science Research Associates (1995)
Principal Investigator, Lawrence
Livermore National Laboratory

Establishment Clause Doctrine and Public Schools
(1986)

Seashore Zoology (1963)

WORKS IN PROGRESS

The Adventures of Dr. Greenstone and Jerrythespider.
The Trilogy: Battle of Top Hat Wood, The Moroccan
Three Murders, and the Case of the Hollow Madonna

All Points of the Compass

Arthur Bacterium and Patty Virus in the Faster Than
The Speed Of Light Adventure Series